Wooing
Miss Whately

Wooing Miss Whately

Meredith Bond

THORNDIKE

CHIVERS

This Large Print edition is published by Thorndike Press®, Waterville, Maine USA and by BBC Audiobooks, Ltd, Bath, England.

Published in 2004 in the U.S. by arrangement with Zebra Books, an imprint of Kensington Publishing Corp.

Published in 2005 in the U.K. by arrangement with Kensington Publishing Corp.

U.S. Hardcover 0-7862-6975-8   (Romance)
U.K. Hardcover 1-4056-3174-0   (Chivers Large Print)

The text of this Large Print edition is unabridged.
Other aspects of the book may vary from the original edition.

Set in 16 pt. Plantin by Myrna S. Raven.

Printed in the United States on permanent paper.

British Library Cataloguing-in-Publication Data available

Library of Congress Cataloging-in-Publication Data

Bond, Meredith.
    Wooing Miss Whately / Meredith Bond.
      p. cm.
    ISBN 0-7862-6975-8 (lg. print : hc : alk. paper)
    1. Administration of estates — Fiction.   2. Americans — England — Fiction.   3. Treasure-trove — Fiction.
4. England — Fiction.   5. Large type books.   I. Title.
PS3602.O6565W66 2004
    813'.6—dc22
                                           2004055393

*In loving memory of my mother,
Nessa Wolfson, who introduced me to the joys
of the Regency and Georgette Heyer.*

One

"You cannot be serious!"

"I assure you, Miss, that I am perfectly serious. I have urgent business which necessitates that I leave immediately."

"And you simply expect me to give up my post chaise to you? Why, in heaven's name, would I want to do that when that would leave *me* stranded here?"

Lord Reath moved further into the room, but had to suppress a curse when he bumped his head on the low, sloping ceiling. "Well, I am sure that you are exhausted from your tiring voyage. You should take the time to rest before you begin the next length of your journey.

"If you would allow me, it would be my pleasure to see to it that you are comfortable. I would be happy to secure for you the finest room in this inn. And then," he slipped in gently, "of course, you would have no need of this post chaise today, which I could use for my own urgent business."

The girl was about to speak again, but he raised his hand.

"And tomorrow, when both you and your maid are completely refreshed and rested, you will be able to get another post chaise or to secure a ticket on the mail coach. It is such a shame that today's was completely full, is it not? What do you say, miss? Will you make a go of it?" Just for good measure he gave her his most charming smile.

The young woman locked her hands together in front of her shabby brown round traveling gown and looked at him silently, as if assessing the situation.

"I think, sir, that *you* may go," she paused, and then leaned forward to emphasize her point, "to hell."

He had extended his hand to her to seal the deal but, at her words, let it drop abruptly.

"Oh, Miss Sara, it wouldn't make much difference to us, now, would it?"

He turned to exchange a look with the lady's maid, who had looked entreatingly at her mistress and then flashed him a quick glance under her lashes.

The lady frowned. "Yes, Annie, it definitely would. We have been delayed long enough, taking two full days just to get in to port. I am not going to delay any further. I promised my aunt we would travel on to her home as soon as we landed at Portsmouth, and I plan on doing just that."

"Of course you should keep to your promise to your aunt," he said, maintaining the smile on his face. "And a fine young lady such as yourself should not have to put up with an inferior inn such as this. I will put you up at the Crown, the finest inn in Portsmouth, and you shall be provided with the most lavish fare that the excellent cook there can prepare. Once you are rested and well fed, you can travel on to your aunt, and she will delight in having you arrive safely and well rested. Surely this will be so much more pleasant than traveling on today."

She paused for a moment. He had won; she was going to give in.

"I do believe that hell might be too good for one such as you," she said, thoughtfully.

He ran a hand through his hair, causing a lock of his straight jet-black hair to fall into his eyes. Brushing it away irritably, he decided that it was time for a change in tactics.

He straightened himself to his full height — which he knew at just over six feet was impressive — and looked down his nose at the petite young woman before him.

"I am sure that your aunt will understand when you explain to her that the Viscount Reath was in need of your conveyance."

The young lady's face darkened, her eyes narrowing and her lovely lips tightening. He braced himself.

"You believe that my aunt will not mind," she said in a dangerously quiet voice, "my being yet another day late? And why, pray, would she be so forgiving? Because you are a viscount?"

"Yes. Because of my position, I have extremely important business I must see to with all haste. I have just arrived from India, and I have matters of state to which I must attend."

Matters of his *estate* rather than of state, he acknowledged to himself, but such a small difference shouldn't be of import.

"I am sure that your aunt, if she is a woman of any sense at all, will understand this when you explain it to her," he concluded.

"I do not know, sir, if my aunt is a woman of sense, for I have not yet met her. But I will tell you this — if she does have any sense, then I expect that she will agree with me that it matters little what rank you are.

"I don't care a fig whether you are a count or a cobbler. If you were the prince, or even that lunatic you call king, I see no reason why your business is any more important than mine. If my aunt can wait another day for my arrival, then surely your business, if you even have any, can as well."

"You are from America, are you?" he asked, making a great effort to keep his voice pleasant.

"Yes, but . . ."

"That explains everything," he said. "You clearly have no idea of the importance of a man in my position. Why one such as you . . ."

"*You* must learn, sir," she said, cutting him off. Her anger was now flaring out from her changeable blue eyes and a flush crept up her lovely heart shaped face. She took a step closer and Reath, to his surprise, found himself retreating.

"*You* must learn that you cannot simply waltz into a room and expect everyone to bow down to you and give you anything you want just because you flash them your perfect smile. The fact that you feel you can use your good looks and inherited title, neither of which you have done anything to deserve, is beyond comprehension.

"It is time you took a page from your

11

American cousins and learn that you must either earn what you want or accept the fate that life hands you, just like everyone else. Now I suggest that you make haste to the innkeeper and secure the best room for yourself before you find that gone as well."

To his utter amazement, the young lady then turned her back on him and proceeded to sit down to drink her now cold tea.

He had been dismissed! The great diplomat Sinclair Stratton, Fourth Viscount Reath, had been dismissed by a little strip of a girl. He looked at the maid, but she was no help, for she was standing there with an expression of helpless disbelief on her face. It was precisely how he felt himself, but, thank God, he had the grace not to show it.

He turned on his heel and left the room, closing the door quietly behind him. Running his hand through his hair in frustration once again, he felt the urge to turn right back around and tell that little chit that she would do better to respect her betters and turn over her post chaise to him.

But he did not.

He took two steps down the hallway toward the common room but then stopped. A smile was twitching at his lips, and before he knew it, his shoulders were shaking with quiet laughter.

He had certainly been put in his place, hadn't he? And by a tiny little nobody! Well, that little nobody certainly had nerve, he had to say that for her. He shook his head and continued on down the hall.

How is it that he was able to convince rajas and nawabs to turn over their kingdoms to the British Empire, but could not convince one girl to turn over her post chaise to him? He almost laughed out loud at that thought, and had to put his hand over his mouth to contain his laughter.

A woman immune to his charm! Why, he had never met such a one before. Never had a female not given him exactly what he wanted when he had flashed her his smile. He wasn't exactly sure whether it was his perfectly straight white teeth or the dimple that appeared in his cheek when he did it, but he just knew that it always worked. Until now.

Ha! But she was not completely immune — hadn't she just said that he couldn't get everything he wanted just because he was handsome?

By gad, what a strong woman! This was a woman, whatever her birth and breeding, who was deserving of his respect. It was almost a shame he would never meet her again. For a woman like that, with a tongue like a whip, would certainly make a stir among the *ton*.

He laughed his way into the common room, shaking his head at the idea of that little firebrand taking the *beau monde* by storm.

Two

As Sara Whately stepped down from the carriage, she smoothed down her crumpled dress, wiped the sweat from her palms at the same time, and took a deep breath. She couldn't decide if she was just nervous at meeting her aunt for the first time, or if she was still upset over her altercation that morning. Perhaps a bit of both, she decided.

The evening sunlight glinted off the imposing facade of her aunt's home. At the sight, her feeling of longing for the comfortable little house on Spruce Street where she had grown up intensified. Her home was just one of a line of brick houses right on the street, all attached, each one no more than twenty feet wide — nothing at all like this vast stone mansion floating in a sea of manicured green lawns and flowering gardens.

She hastily reminded herself of her father's numerous assurances that his sister was the soul of amiability. But her father, good-natured and trusting, had never been the best judge of people.

The heavily ornamented door opened as

if of its own volition. A tall, thin man stepped out and bowed to her. "Miss Whately, I presume?" he said in a disconcertingly deep voice.

Sara gathered her wits quickly and lifted her chin a notch. "That is correct. I am here to see Lady Darlington. I believe I am expected."

"Yes, Miss. Right this way. A footman will see to your trunks."

He led the way inside and up a grand marble staircase. Opening the first door on their right, he stepped into the room and intoned, "Miss Whately, my lady."

Sara resisted the urge to wipe her palms against her dress again and instead tightly clasped her hands together in front of her as she walked in.

She had an impression of a light, airy room with bright yellow walls dense with paintings. But her eyes were fixed on the lady who bustled toward her, a broad welcoming smile on her face.

So this was her aunt! Her gray silk morning dress, cinched just below her bosom by a wide lavender ribbon, bespoke her dowager status, but the rich chestnut curls which softly framed her face gave her a very young look. And, with a rush of relief, Sara saw in her face echoes of the features of her own beloved father, as well as a sweetness and simple good humor that was also very much his.

She took Sara's hands in her own and pressed her cheek to hers. Sara inhaled and smelled roses — such a refreshing change from the damp smell of the carriage and the salty smell of the sea.

"Welcome, my dear Sara! Welcome to Darlington! Welcome to England!"

"Thank you, ma'am. I am very happy to be here." Sara gave her the best smile she could manage and then swallowed audibly.

"I must admit to you," Lady Darlington said, holding Sara at arms' length and searching her face, "I have been very nervous all day about meeting you. Is that not right, Alston?"

She turned to face a middle-aged gentleman who had been standing by the window. Sara had not even noticed that he was there until her aunt had spoken to him, but now he came forward. He looked exactly as she had imagined all gentleman farmers to look, wearing buckskin breeches, a blue coat of superfine, and a simple white neckcloth tied carelessly under his chin. He too wore a large welcoming smile, but he stopped short of Sara and bowed formally.

"Indeed, Miss Whately, your aunt has been flitting here and there, unable to stay in any one place for more than a minute all afternoon. I am sure that it was nerves which kept her in constant motion."

Lady Darlington giggled. "Oh dear, how true, how true."

"Deanna, will you not do the honor of introducing us? I know who Miss Whately is, but I believe she is wondering who I am." The severity of his words were softened by the smile which crinkled at the corners of his mouth and eyes.

"Oh, of course, how forgetful I am!" Lady Darlington turned to her niece. "Sara, may I present my very good friend and neighbor, Justin, Baron Alston?"

Sara curtsied. "I am pleased to meet you, sir."

"The pleasure is mine. I hear you are come from the wilds of America," he said with a grand gesture and laughter in his voice.

Sara raised her chin and straightened her back. "Not the wilds, sir. I have come from Philadelphia."

The smile left Lord Alston's face for a moment, and he flicked a look at Lady Darlington. When he turned back to

18

Sara, his mouth was smiling, but his eyes no longer were.

"Please forgive me. I did not know from whence in America you had come. I must warn you that not many people here know the degree of civilization that has been established in Philadelphia."

"Do you, sir?" Sara retorted.

"I have heard, Miss Whately."

"I do hope that your journey was pleasant, Sara?" her aunt asked, interrupting the awkward tension that was rapidly growing in the room.

"It was, ma'am, until I reached Portsmouth. Then I had a rather disagreeable encounter with some viscount."

"Some viscount? I do not understand."

"This odious man behaved exactly the way I had feared an English gentleman would act. First, he expected me to simply give up my post chaise — the last one available — to him simply because he had a title. Then, when I refused, he tried to intimidate me with his size. He was enormous! He filled the entire private parlor I had secured for myself. Finally, when that failed, he turned on his charm. He had a beautiful smile and flashed his gray eyes at me. Clearly, he expected to me to just give in to him because he was handsome!"

"Lud! What a picture you paint, my dear! What did you do?"

"Why, I told him precisely what I thought of him and his grand title and then I sent him on his way. After having met this pompous gentleman with his lofty pretensions, I must say, I was never so proud of my papa for having given up his title. The nerve of these English noblemen! They all think that they are better than everyone else simply because of the happenstance of birth."

Lord Alston cleared his throat, and it suddenly occurred to Sara that there were two English nobles standing directly in front of her. She felt her face heat and was sure that she had turned bright red.

"Oh dear, I . . . I did not mean . . . Aunt Deanna, Lord Alston, I, er . . ." Sara took a deep breath and managed to whisper, "Present company excluded, of course."

Her aunt did not look terribly pleased, but she forced a smile on to her face. "Of course, my dear. We know that you were not referring to all titled Englishmen." She thought for a moment. "I do wonder, though, who it could have been who was so incredibly rude to you. You don't remember his name?"

"No, ma'am. Only that he had black hair

and slashing black eyebrows over the most striking gray eyes, and a smile to . . . well, he was very handsome." Sara felt her face heat once again, only this time not from embarrassment. "Oh, and he clearly felt himself to be very important, saying that he had just come from India and had pressing matters of state to which he had to attend — as if I would believe such gammon!"

"India?" Lady Darlington turned to Lord Alston. "Justin, you don't . . . you wouldn't think it was . . ."

Lord Alston was quiet for a moment, his eyes searching Lady Darlington's as they shared some unspoken communication. "Yes, Deanna. I am sorry, but it does indeed sound like it was."

All the color left Lady Darlington's face and she reached out a hand for support. Sara grasped it. She quickly moved next to her aunt and guided her to the sofa nearby.

"Aunt, are you all right?" Sara said, sitting down next to her. She grabbed a publication from off of the table next to her and began waving it in front of her aunt's face.

"Yes. Yes, my dear. You are very kind. I just felt a trifle dizzy for a moment there. But I shall be better directly, I assure you."

Lord Alston sat down on her other side, concern filling his eyes. "Deanna, do not worry so. He will do nothing," he said gently.

"No, I am not worried about him — but society?"

Lord Alston frowned for a moment. "Their memory is not so long, I assure you."

He then turned to Sara. "Miss Whately, I am sorry that you had such a very unfortunate encounter, but truly you must learn to watch what you say and to whom. I understand that you meant nothing personal toward myself and your lady aunt when speaking of titled persons, but others will not be so forgiving.

"You clearly have inherited the famous Whately temper. You must be very careful, or you will soon find yourself completely without friends."

"Oh, Alston! You are not being helpful. As if any of this was Sara's fault." The color was returning to Lady Darlington's face, and she patted Sara's arm fondly. "You must pay no mind to him. What a horrid thing to say! Without friends, indeed."

"I say this in the spirit of friendship and concern for one who is soon to be brought out into polite society, Deanna. She must learn to watch her tongue."

"And so she will. I am sure that Sara is a properly brought up young lady."

Sara did not say anything, but hoped that she would not prove her aunt wrong.

"Now, Alston, if you will be so kind as to leave. Sara and I are going to sit and have a nice little coze, just the two of us."

A small smile began forming on Lord Alston's face as he rose. "Miss Whately, do you also have a habit of telling your friends what they may and may not do, and when they must leave your presence?"

"Yes. I must admit that I do," Sara replied in complete seriousness.

"Of course she does! She is my niece, after all. I am sure that we will find many things in common," said Lady Darlington, immediately coming to Sara's defense.

Making a shooing motion, she said again, "Now do go away, Alston. Oh, and on your way out, tell Coddles to send in some tea."

Lord Alston accepted his dismissal in good humor, gave them a small bow, and then left.

Lady Darlington turned back to Sara. "There. Now that man is gone, we can finally talk."

"He is a very close friend of yours, ma'am?"

"Alston? Oh yes, of course. He and I have been friends for years. He was with me when Darlington died. Don't know what I would have done without him all these years. Honestly." Her aunt surreptitiously wiped at the corner of her eye with her handkerchief. "But enough about him. And I want you to forget all about that horrible viscount and Portsmouth and your journey. Just tell me about yourself."

She took Sara's hands in hers again and looked at her expectantly.

"I . . . I don't know what to tell you, ma'am."

"Well, first of all you must stop calling me ma'am. Aunt will be good enough. Aunt Deanna, if you wish. And tell me about your father. How is he? I can never tell from those letters he writes. They are so . . . so literary. I can't make head or tails of what he is trying to say, if anything."

Sara smiled. Her father's writing style was, in fact, very difficult to decipher. Sara had been reading it her whole life and so was used to it, but she could clearly see how her aunt would have trouble.

"My father is well, thank you. I left him in the care of our neighbor, Mrs. Cartwright. We have no housekeeper, you know, and I took our only maid with me, for he would not hear of my traveling alone."

"Absolutely correct. You cannot go anywhere alone, my dear. I am sure that you know that," her aunt concurred.

Sara was silent for a moment. She was sure her aunt meant she could not go on long journeys alone. She turned her mind back to her father.

Gently pulling her hands away from her aunt's grasp, she clasped them tightly together in her lap. She had never felt so worried before, but she had never been away from her father before, either. She felt completely helpless and did not like the feeling at all.

Thousands of miles away, she was completely unable to ensure that her father was being properly taken care of. Even if she were to write to see how he went on, it would take weeks, if not months, for a letter to reach him, if it did at all with the hostilities growing between America and Great Britain. She still felt a enormous amount of relief that she had reached British shores safely.

"I do hope he is all right. He is rather lost in his work most of the time, and probably would not remember to eat or sleep if someone were not there to remind him."

"Do not worry, my dear. I am sure he is fine." Lady Darlington looked very concerned and gently patted Sara's hands. "I am so sorry. I did not mean to upset you."

Sara swallowed hard and pasted a smile on her face. "It is all right. I am being silly, of course. I am sure he is greatly relieved to be out from under my thumb and is enjoying his newfound freedom." The words came out of her mouth, but not her heart.

Lady Darlington stood up. "I believe I have been terribly selfish, Sara. You must be exhausted from your trip, and here I have kept you gabbing. Let me show you to your room so that you may rest a spell before supper."

"That is not necessary, Aunt, I assure you . . ." Sara began.

"Pish-tosh! There is no need to stand on formality with me, my dear. I am your family. I can see in your eyes that you are ready to drop."

Three

Reath urged his horses to a faster pace. The perfectly matched pair were prime bits of blood, and his father's curricle was built for speed. If for no other reason than getting this equipage, the delay in his trip caused by stopping at his family seat was worthwhile.

Appreciating the sight of strong muscles rippling under the horses' sleek brown coats, Reath found himself momentarily distracted from his driving. They really were an excellently matched pair. If it was one thing his father had known about, it was prime-blood horses. He had always had the best, and Reath took after his father in this one way — he truly appreciated a fine horse. And two were even better.

On the other hand, there was his last mount — the nag he had finally been able to borrow to get him as far as the next posting house along the road. He laughed at the contrast. In fact, he had been quite relieved that the beast had been able to carry him so far — a sorrier looking creature Reath had never ventured to mount.

His father's excellent pair was able to

maintain impressive speed, and Reath thrilled in the feeling as he expertly handled the ribbons. The drive along the main roads had been easy, but now he kept a strong hand on the reins as he guided the pair through the narrow winding lane. Such speed and power was heady to one who had been cooped up on a ship for the past six months.

The light curricle swung around a tight corner, one wheel nearly lifting off the ground.

On the other side of the blind curve, a girl was slowly riding down the middle of the road. Within moments he would be upon her.

Reath acted quickly, pulling hard on the reins and veering off to one side at the same time. The horses managed to move over just enough so that he missed the girl by a hair.

He brought the frightened pair to a standstill, and realized that both he and the horses were trembling at their near miss.

But he had no time to dwell on his own feelings. Jumping down and running back to the girl, he found her sitting, winded and shocked, on the ground where her horse had thrown her before bolting back to his stables.

"Are you all right?" he asked, kneeling down in front of her.

And then he sucked in his breath as he recognized the young woman from Portsmouth.

Sara looked up into the gray eyes of the gentleman from Portsmouth. Just as quickly as his eyes had widened with surprise at seeing her, they had softened with concern.

"I am going to feel for broken bones," he said, reaching down to feel her ankle.

The heat from his hand shot up her leg. Instinctively, Sara pulled back out of his reach.

"How dare you!" she exclaimed, as anger flooded over her. How could this man presume to look so concerned? He certainly had exhibited no such feeling when he had tried to convince her to give up her post chaise to him. If it had been anyone else, Sara might have understood the worry for her well-being. But no, not this man.

He pulled his hand back, and then abruptly stood up. "I am sorry, I meant no offense. I was only checking —"

"Yes, I know very well what you were checking! It would have been better, sir, had you checked your horses before flying around that turn."

He stared down at her for a minute, and then his eyes narrowed. With an edge in his voice, he bit out, "Well, what fool rides down the middle of the road? You are damned lucky that I am such an excellent driver."

"Excellent driver! You nearly ran me down!"

"Yes, and had I not been expert in the handling of the ribbons, you would be a lot worse off than you are now!"

The nerve of the man! Once again, he was trying to turn the situation to his own advantage when he was the one clearly at fault. She would not allow herself to be manipulated by this arrogant English peer.

The first step toward gaining control of the situation, though, was to see if she could actually stand.

Tentatively, she flexed one leg and then the other. Satisfied that nothing was broken, she made a move to get up.

Immediately, his commanding voice arrested her movement. "No. You should not get up just yet."

Sara looked up at the man, still looming over her. "What, am I supposed to just stay sitting here in the middle of the road?"

She resolved to ignore him. She did not allow herself to be dictated to by anyone. She never had and she never would. But as she put weight on her foot, it twisted under her and she winced at the sudden stab of pain.

At once, he reached out and held her elbow, guiding her back to the ground. "Really, Miss, you should wait a few minutes before you try to stand."

Sara was about to snap at him again when she realized that he wasn't trying to thwart her, but actually to help. His handsome face wore an expression of concern . . . and perhaps a trace of guilt.

Sara found herself strangely moved. It was clear that he was concerned about her, beyond his natural remorse.

But why?

No one had ever worried much about her, not since her mother had died when she was six. Her parents' friends and neighbors had rallied around at that time, and had tried to show their sorrow and consideration. But their attentiveness had waned with time, especially as little Sara had proven herself to be capable and strong.

Sara had quickly taken her mother's place and become the hub around which her household was run. By the time she was nine, she had taken complete charge of everything, instructing Annie and the daily maid to clean the house, prepare meals from the little that they could afford, and take care of her ever-impractical father. She had done it all, uncomplainingly managing their household for the last decade.

She was the one who cared for others. And yet here was this strange man who wanted to take care of *her*. It was too odd even to be considered.

"I will do as I please," she said with a lift of her chin, and then once again tried to stand.

He put his hand around her back. "At least let me help you this time."

She flinched at his touch, but was moved again by the concern in his voice. Biting her lip, she nodded her head. Taking his arm, she rose to her feet.

It was still too soon. As she stood, she felt her head reel, and her legs seemed to give way under her. She leaned against him, needing his support.

It was so tempting to rest her head against him and allow his strong arms to wrap themselves around her to hold her close and care for her. She could feel his hard muscles, the power in his masculine body. Why not allow him to take care of everything?

And he smelled so good, she thought dazedly. She had noticed his scent when they had met in Portsmouth. It was spicy and foreign. In Portsmouth there had been a tinge of the smell of salt from the sea, but now that had been replaced by leather and sweat. How could just a man's scent make her heart race so?

No! She would not give in to this man. She would be strong, just as she always had. She was not a simpering miss to rely on a man to help her out of every difficult situation.

"Thank you," she said, forcing herself to pull back. "I am a little light-headed, I'm afraid."

"Naturally. Come and sit on the soft grass for a moment."

He began to lead her toward the side of the road where the grass was thickest.

It did look enticing. And it would be so nice to sit down and rest a moment, sheltered in his concern — just until she could get her bearings back.

She fought against the inclination. She would not show any weakness — and certainly not in front of this man, who clearly thought nothing of managing her life.

"No. No, it is all right. I am fine, really," Sara said. She looked down and brushed the worst of the dust and dirt from her dress.

"Still in a hurry to get to your important business?" she asked, finally looking up at him, trying to put more distance between them. The sooner she was away from this man, the sooner she would no longer feel this ridiculous need for him to care for her. Yet somehow, her question came out sounding less combative than she had intended it to be.

He raised one slashing eyebrow. "Er . . . yes."

"Well, do not let me keep you, sir. Goodness knows I have delayed you enough already."

"I cannot simply leave you here all alone without a means of conveyance. Your horse has disappeared, I'm afraid."

She looked around and noticed that he was quite right. "Damn," she said. She was trapped. She had no way of getting back to her aunt's house.

Then she suddenly realized that she had cursed out loud, and felt her face heat. Her father had lectured her on her language after she had tried using a few of the more colorful expressions she had learned in the market. But she still had not rid herself of the bad habit of using one or two choice words when the situation demanded it.

She stole a look at the gentleman to see if he had heard her. He had. But thankfully, his lips were twitching with suppressed mirth.

Reath tried to hold back his laughter. He was aware that if there was one thing that would infuriate this intriguing, maddening girl again, it was a show of levity. And he did not want to disturb their brief, enjoyable truce.

She, however, had clearly noticed his suppressed amusement, and an answering smile flit on and off of her face.

So she did have a sense of humor! There was more to this spirited young lady than met the eye. And he could not help but notice that even this brief smile lit up her face in a most becoming way.

Yet when she had been sitting on the ground, there been a moment when some deep sadness had flickered in her eyes. He could not imagine what he had said or done to cause this, but he was glad to see that she had pushed it away and was now able to laugh, or at least smile.

"I do seem to be in a bit of a fix now,"

she acknowledged. But just as she said this, a small gig came around the same turn in the road. It pulled to a halt and a gentleman leaped out.

"Miss Whately, is everything all right?"

"Ah, Lord Alston. What excellent timing. Are you perhaps on your way to . . ."

"Are you in need of assistance, Miss Whately?" Lord Alston interrupted, a frown on his brow as he looked from Sara to Reath.

"Yes, please. It seems my horse has bolted and I have no other means of getting home."

"I would be happy to drive you," Reath said quickly. "It is, after all, my fault that you lost your horse."

She dismissed him with a wave her hand, saying, "Thank you, sir, but I am sure that Lord Alston will not mind, as he is already in the vicinity."

"No, I would not mind in the least. Thank you for your offer, sir. I will take care of the young lady from here on."

There was little Reath could do or say. He bowed gracefully and then helped her into the gig.

"Thank you," she said, looking into his eyes. Reath felt a loss. Her eyes, which he had noted before as so expressive, were now shuttered against him.

Lord Alston snapped the reins and then, with the briefest nod, took off down the road.

Reath shook his head. The young lady was indeed an odd creature. Any other woman would have been in hysterics over their near accident. Why, even a man would have been shaken. But this girl had just stood up, brushed herself off, and gone on her way almost as if nothing had happened.

Reath climbed back into his curricle. Unwinding the reins from the brake, he could not help but remember the feel of her neat ankle beneath his hand as he had attempted to feel for broken bones. And thanks to her brief spell of light-headedness, he also had had no need to wonder about the rest of her slender form. The way she had leaned against him been extremely intimate.

For a moment he had felt as if he truly knew her — the lilt of her unusual colonial accent, her distinctive rose-and-lemon scent, the sensuous feel of her soft curves.

He could not help but smile as he continued on his way. He knew that a true gentleman should not have enjoyed the last. But indeed he had.

★ ★ ★

Reath slowed down and pulled his team to a halt in front of the door of Wyncort Hall. A groom came running from the stables to take control of the horses and a large portly man, who Reath supposed to be the butler despite his casual attire, stepped from the house.

Jumping down, he gave brief instructions to the groom before turning toward the house. A small skinny man with a little mustache had joined the butler, and now was bowing low to him.

"My lord. Welcome. Welcome to Wyncort. I do hope your journey was pleasant. We are very pleased to see you here, my lord."

Reath strode into the house, the little man following at his heels like a puppy. "Thank you, Lipking. No, I did *not* have a pleasant journey. In fact, it was fraught with one problem after another, but I am finally here."

Reath stopped and faced the butler, waiting for an introduction.

"Ah, yes. My lord, this is Tate, the caretaker of the estate. He and his wife have been working very hard to ready the house for your arrival."

Reath nodded as the man bowed to him.

"I am sorry your journey was not easier," the solicitor said, leading Reath into a room just off the main entranceway. "I do hope that you will find everything here as you requested, my lord."

The room Reath was led into had clearly once been the library, but now the shelves that lined the three walls were completely denuded of their books. The only furniture in the room was two old wing chairs of dried, cracked leather sitting by a large ornately carved fireplace, and a large oak desk and chair facing the bare window at the far end of the room. Since the room was a fair-sized one, these meager furnishings did nothing to show off its advantages.

"Could you not have provided a little more furniture, Lipking?" Reath asked, stopping briefly just inside the room.

"I . . . I am sorry, my lord. I had not thought to purchase furniture, as it was my understanding that you were not going to take up residence," the little man answered.

"No, but this is too sparse. I do not want it to be quite so evident that no one has lived here for the past ten years."

"Yes, my lord." Lipking went over to the desk where he had some papers spread out and made a note to himself. With a glance up at Reath, he turned a slight shade of pink and then gathered up his papers carefully, but quickly, and removed them from the desk to the case at his feet.

Reath caught sight of a decanter and two glasses sitting on one of the empty shelves and helped himself to a liberal glass of wine. After swallowing half of it at one go, he was pleasantly surprised at the quality and refilled his glass. He then made himself as comfortable as possible on the chair facing the desk, where Lipking was still shuffling his papers.

"Now tell me what progress you have made here."

"Well, my lord, I am afraid not much since I last communicated with you. I have still been unable to locate Lord Wynsham. It is as if he has completely disappeared. After his move to America twenty years ago, no one has seen or heard from him."

"No one at all? Is that not a little odd, Lipking?"

"Indeed, my lord. Aside from thinking that perhaps he has fallen victim to the red Indians, I really have no clue as what may have happened to him."

"Did you check all the major cities, as well as the countryside?"

"My lord, I have had men searching for

his whereabouts for over a year now. They have searched throughout the colony, everywhere Englishmen have been known to settle. They can find no one named Wynsham."

Reath took a long sip from his drink. "Did he have any friends or siblings who might still be in contact with him?"

"I have looked into that, my lord. The only sibling he has is a sister, Lady Darlington. I have written her two letters, my lord, but so far she has not replied."

"Perhaps you would do best to try contacting Lord Darlington. I don't suppose a woman can entirely be trusted to understand the importance of responding to business correspondence."

"I am afraid he is deceased, my lord. Has been these past three years."

"Damn." Reath ran his hand through his hair. "Well then, perhaps if I pay her a visit I might be able to learn something. Do you have her direction, Lipking?"

"Yes, my lord. Actually, Darlington is the neighboring estate here, but I am certain she has already returned to her town house on Leicester Square for the Season."

Reath nodded. Yes, of course, the Season must have just begun. He wondered just how long the *ton*'s memory was. Would he be able to start with a clean reputation once again, or would he be condemned from the very beginning because of his youthful foolishness? He did not relish the idea of returning to society, but at least now he was older and wiser. And it was imperative that he find Lady Darlington and somehow discover her brother's whereabouts.

Four

"That cow-handed, beef-witted . . . toad!" Sara said without preamble as she walked through the door into her aunt's drawing room.

"Sara! Please, watch your language!" Her aunt placed the embroidery she had been stitching on the table next to her. A bright smile lit her face as Lord Alston entered the room behind Sara. "Hello, Justin."

"Hello, Deanna." Lord Alston gave a kiss to Lady Darlington's outstretched hand.

Sara watched the interplay, still seething inside. Her anger at herself for being so weak still rankled. She was also still annoyed with the viscount for reprimanding her for riding in the middle of the road. What was even worse was that he was right.

But what right did he have to chastise her when he himself had been driving entirely too fast?

She did reluctantly admit to herself that he had been quite magnificent in the way he had averted disaster. But she was not about let him know how he had amazed her with his driving prowess, especially not after he had just felt her leg in the most intimate way. No, she had been absolutely right to be rude to him.

And she had been grateful for Lord Alston's silence all the way home. He had not asked her the most obvious questions, perhaps knowing that he would learn everything once they had reached Darlington.

Now that they had done so, Sara allowed her anger to dominate all her other feelings.

Her aunt could probably sense her anger all the way across the room. "Sara, you are covered with dirt! What happened to you? And why, pray, are you cursing like a sailor?"

"What happened? That idiot viscount just nearly ran me over, that is what happened." Sara forced herself to keep a calm tone of voice.

"Which idiot — er, which viscount? Justin?" Her aunt looked to Lord Alston for clarification and support.

"Was that the gentleman you met in Portsmouth?" Lord Alston asked Sara.

"Yes. It was the very same man."

Lord Alston gave her aunt a very disturbed look.

"It wasn't . . ." she began.

Lord Alston gave her aunt an almost imperceptible nod.

Her aunt blanched and dropped back down onto her chair. "Can you tell us what happened, Sara?" she said quietly.

Sara looked from Lord Alston to her aunt. She could not help but wonder if her aunt was upset over her accident, or the man who had caused it.

"The man I met in Portsmouth just nearly ran me down with his curricle and pair," she said, but without the same fire that she had felt when she first entered the room.

"He nearly ran you down? I do not understand," her aunt said, still looking rather pale.

"Yes. He was driving much too fast around a turn in the road and nearly hit me. My horse threw me and then bolted. I do hope the horse returned here unharmed."

"I shall check in the stables in a bit," Alston offered.

"Thank you, Justin. Are you all right, Sara? Were you hurt? Shall I call for the doctor?"

"No. Thank you, Aunt. I am fine. Just

tired and a little shaken," Sara said, actually beginning to feel a bit better. She sat down at the edge of the sofa.

"Well, of course you are. And quite dirty too. You must go directly up to your room. I will send one of the maids up with a nice hot bath for you. It will be make you feel much more the thing."

Sara nodded, knowing her aunt was right, but the thought of getting up again and climbing the stairs was not very appealing now that she had sat down.

Her aunt had turned to Lord Alston. "We must leave as soon as possible," she said, her voice sharp with anxiety. "You know that we must leave at once."

Lady Darlington stood, picked up her embroidery as if to leave with it, and then stopped and put it down again.

"Justin, you will accompany us, will you not? You promised you would escort us to London." Lady Darlington moved to her friend and laid her hand gently on his arm. She looked up at him with a pleading expression in her eyes that was not difficult for Sara to see, and clearly impossible for Lord Alston to resist.

Alston placed his hand over hers and gave it a reassuring pat. "Yes, of course I will, Deanna. When do you think you could be ready to go?"

Relief showed in the way she stood back from him. "Two — no, three days. There is much to be done, but I think I can manage it in three days."

"Very well. I will make the arrangements."

"Thank you." Lady Darlington held out her hand to her friend and smiled up at him as he took it. He allowed his lips to linger a moment as he kissed the back of her hand.

Sara felt that her presence had been forgotten, and although she found watching this touching scene fascinating, she thought she had best make her exit now before anything else happened. She had never witnessed such intimacy before and it made her a little uncomfortable.

"I . . . I believe I will go up for that bath now, Aunt Deanna. Thank you, sir, for bringing me back home. If you will excuse me?" She gave a quick curtsy and then walked from the room without looking back. She was sure that her aunt had been blushing delicately as she had walked by, but she had deliberately kept her eyes on the floor.

Sara sighed as Annie poured in yet another kettle full of hot water into her bath. The scent of her aunt's floral soap and the rose water that Annie had added to her bath gave her a feeling of utter contentment. If only she could stay here and not think of anything else. But there were so many things for her to think and worry about. There was the viscount, Aunt Deanna's reaction to hearing about him, Lord Alston's meaningful exchange of looks with her aunt, and, most of all, the whole purpose of her being in England.

"Annie, we are going to be in trouble if I don't act quickly," Sara said, almost reluctantly.

"Why is that, Miss Sara?" Annie asked, soaping her mistress's back.

"Aunt Deanna said we were to leave for London in only three days' time. That means that I no longer have the leisure I had hoped to have to find out more about that rogue who owns Wyncort." She slid under the water for a moment to rinse off the soap and wet her head so that Annie could wash her hair.

"I did find out today, from my aunt's groom, that no one has lived there for the past ten years, aside from a caretaker and his wife." She wiped the water and some soap from her eyes as Annie massaged the lemon hair tonic into her hair.

"So at least I won't have to worry about running into that rogue. And the groom also told me that the caretakers have been notoriously lax, spending more time at the pub and their daughter's house in town than they have at the estate."

"Close your eyes," Annie said as she dumped another kettle full of warm water on to Sara's head. "I still don't like it, Miss Sara. Why can't you just find a nice man to marry, like your father said?"

"I will not marry for money, Annie. I simply will not do it," Sara said, after she had wiped the water from her face once again. "Now I just need to get into that house."

Annie sighed loudly. "You just won't give up, will you, Miss Sara?"

Sara wrung the excess water from her waist-length hair, then took the towel Annie had had warming in front of the fire.

"No, Annie, I won't. My entire future and that of my father rests on my getting into that house. How could you possibly expect me to give that up?"

The following morning, before her aunt could enlist her help with the packing, Sara went out riding. She was determined to at least see Wyncort, if not get inside before she left for London.

Following the directions given by her aunt's groom, Sara rode around the newly planted fields of wheat and barley to reach the far end of the property. There, along the boundary between Darlington and Wyncort, lay the dense wood her father had written about in his darker moments. She had read her father's stories of

"The deep, dark wood that would
ere swallow a man a night,
before spitting him out again
but only half a man for fear and fright."

Sara had had nightmares after reading about this forest and now that she faced it, she could barely bring herself to enter it.

She stood in indecision, looking at the dark, forbidding trees that quickly thickened, giving no indication of where they might end. A light breeze ruffed through her hair and the morning sun was just beginning to dispel the cool of the night. She looked back behind her at the green open field of young plants and her aunt's large yet stately house beyond. The well-manicured lawns that she had scoffed at only two days ago now seemed so warm and friendly in comparison to the ominous forest.

Sara squared her shoulders, lifted her chin and stepped forward into the wood. Following a faint path, she wound her way through the damp trees as quickly as possible. Everything was cool, dark, and still. Sara's skin prickled at the silence, and yet she feared any sound.

A rustle nearby made Sara jump. Were there animals in the forest? She had not thought of that, but now she supposed that there were.

Sara stopped, now truly frightened. She half turned to go back to the safety of her aunt's estate. No! She was not a coward. She turned back to the path resolutely and continued on toward Wyncort.

Sara had to concentrate on where she was walking. Bushes and young trees had grown and stretched across the path, making it difficult to keep to it. She could not afford to get lost, for if she did so, she knew that she could be winding her way through the forest for hours, if not the entire day. But if she just stayed on the path it would not be far to the other side.

She felt a sharp tug on her skirt and stopped suddenly, rigid with fear. Keeping her eyes on the ground, she turned around slowly — and saw that her dress had caught on a broken branch her feet had just skirted.

Sara breathed again. After carefully freeing her dress, she held her skirt up to an indelicate height so that she could proceed more easily. She desperately wanted to turn back and escape to the safe familiarity of her aunt's estate. But, swallowing hard, she forced herself to go forward, deeper into the woods.

The semidarkness made the wood even more cold and menacing, knowing as she did that the sun was shining outside of the forest. Only here and there did rays of sunlight break through the trees, creating shafts of golden light. She moved as quickly as she could from one patch of light to the next.

The trees began to thin, the light grew stronger, and Sara could feel the chill that had seeped into her bones begin to recede. She quickened her step so that she was out of the forest and stepping onto a carpet of soft grass.

She stopped and took a deep breath. The thick sweet smell of roses filled her senses, as did the sense of relief at being finally out of the forest.

Following her nose, she walked through

a break in a tall hedge, into an overgrown rose garden where roses of every shade of pink vied with each other for prominence. Despite the fact that they clearly had not been tended for some time, the roses continued to thrive, if a bit wildly.

Sara slowly walked through the garden, enjoying the nearly overwhelming scent of the flowers. Her grandparents had walked these paths, she thought, and her father had played here as a child. She could barely imagine her dearly beloved gray-haired papa as a young boy, and nearly laughed at her fanciful thoughts.

She took herself in hand after that, focusing her mind on the task at hand. She was here for a purpose, not just for a walk through a pretty garden, she reprimanded herself. She turned toward the house.

Wide white marble steps led to a large patio that stretched across the back of the house. At either end of the patio were two sets of double French doors.

Sara stopped and peered inside, cupping her hands around her eyes so that she could see into the darkened rooms. There was a long grand ballroom through one set of doors and what looked like a dining room or breakfast parlor through the other set.

She tried the handles of all the doors, but they were firmly locked. She supposed she shouldn't be surprised, but it was frustrating nonetheless. She was here at Wyncort, a place she had only dreamed of, and yet she could not get inside. She wished she had a more concrete plan or even had more time to make one. She turned to walk toward the side of the house, thinking that perhaps there would be an open window or side door somewhere, but just at that moment, a voice startled her.

"Hey, what are you doing there?" A large, roughly dressed man carrying an ax over his shoulder rounded the corner of the house and started toward her.

Sara turned and ran. She ran as fast as her legs could carry her through the rose garden and back into the wood. She made it through the forest in half the time it had taken her the first time, for she ran as if the devil himself were chasing her.

As she bolted out into the bright sunlight once more, she almost forgot that she had tethered her horse to a nearby tree. She came to a halt, panting and clutching at her side where it ached from running.

She was nearly positive that the man had not followed her into the wood, but she didn't want to take any chances. She led her horse to a fallen log, mounted and then took off at a good pace for Darlington. She wondered if people could be hung for trespassing.

Five

Once again, as Sara approached her aunt's house, the door opened of its own accord.

"Lady Darlington wishes to see you immediately, Miss Whately," Coddles said as if pronouncing a death sentence.

Sara thanked him and then went up to the drawing room where her aunt was sitting at the sofa writing something.

"Oh, Sara, thank goodness you are back."

"I was just out for a ride, Aunt Deanna," Sara said, coming over to her.

"Yes, well, there is simply too much to do. Packing and getting everything ready for our move to London . . . and then we have to be ready to leave in only three days!" her aunt looked like she was ready to burst into tears of frustration.

Sara sat down at the edge of the sofa next to her aunt and put a comforting hand on her arm. "Aunt Deanna, I have been running my father's household for years. If there is anything I can do to help, I will be more than happy to do so."

Aunt Deanna smiled at her and patted

her hand. "I was hoping I would be able to count on you."

She sighed and then handed Sara the paper she had been writing on. "This is a list of all that needs to be done."

Sara looked down the list of about fifteen items.

"Aunt Deanna, if you would make most of the decisions as to precisely what you would like to take with you, I will see that it is all packed and loaded."

Aunt Deanna looked very relieved. "Thank you, my dear. With your help, we will be ready to leave so much earlier than if I had to do all of this by myself. In fact, I am certain that I would not be able to do it."

Sara spent the next three days tirelessly seeing to the packing of the household. Initially, there were a few discreetly raised eyebrows among the staff. But her good cheer, self-confidence, and obvious knowledge quickly won them over. Very soon the maids and footmen were naturally coming to her, rather than to Lady Darlington, with their questions and problems.

Sara, on her part, was shocked at all that her aunt expected to take with her to London. Furniture, household goods, food, and much of her aunt's extensive wardrobe had to be all carefully packed and loaded into wagons and carts. Inventories of the silver and linens had to be seen to. And finally, instructions for a thorough cleaning of the house by the remaining staff, which would take place after they had left, had to be arranged.

On their last evening after dinner, her aunt sat back, satisfied. "Thank you so much for working so very hard, Sara. I can hardly believe that everything is ready for our journey so quickly. Without your assistance, my dear niece, I am sure I would not have been able to accomplish so much in such a short period."

Lord Alston, who had stopped by to judge if they were in fact ready to leave the following day, concurred. "Miss Whately, I have to say that I have never seen your aunt packed and ready to move to London so quickly. It surely must be your good influence and work that has produced this miracle."

Sara shook her head. "Oh no, sir. Indeed, it was Aunt Deanna's excellent organization. I merely followed her orders and saw that things were carried out as she wished."

Lord Alston winked at her and then nodded gravely. "As you say."

Sara could not help but smile back, but refrained from giggling.

Reath sat back in his desk chair and rubbed the back of his neck. He had been poring over these account books for the entire morning. It was incredibly dull work, and he wasn't entirely sure why he was doing it. The steward had been running the estate entirely alone for long enough that he certainly would know what he was doing. Lipking, however, had felt adamant that the books be looked over for any irregularities. Reath couldn't find any.

If anything, the steward had not spent as much money as he should have in maintaining the estate. All of the tenants' homes needed new roofs, one field needed draining; and, during his tour of the house the two days previously, Reath had seen a number of windows with broken glass. And, from unfortunate personal experience, he knew that the chimneys were in desperate need of cleaning.

The tour of the house had been rather uncomfortable, in more ways than one. Mrs. Tate had led him throughout the entire house — from the cellars that had enough space in them to hold the finest collection of wine anyone could want, to the attics that had probably once been filled with nearly a century's worth of things saved from the Wynshams, who had owned this house since Tudor times.

It was not only the age of the house that disturbed him, however. It was the beauty of it as well. The old marble staircase that rose majestically from the entryway with its intricate wrought iron railing. The ballroom that reminded him of the grand rooms his father had told him about from his visit to Versailles and the court of Louis XVI. But most of all, there had been the echoes, in his mind, of children's laughter in the nurseries and through the long hallway of the gallery. He laughed at his fanciful imaginings, but in his heart he knew that this was just the type of home he wanted for himself.

It was a home. Not at all like the formal house where he was raised, where one did not raise one's voice in laughter or exuberance of any kind. Wyncort was warm, even without so many of its paintings, decorations and furniture, for the walls themselves spoke of the laughter and the love that had lived within them. Where Rathergreen Hall was modern and stately, Wyncort was old and comfortable. It had a history and it was a happy one.

Someday, Reath thought to himself, leaning back in his chair. Someday he would own a home like this, where the sound of children's laughter would ring throughout the house.

He looked down at the books in front of him. But not now, and not this home. This home belonged to someone else, and he was determined to return it to them. Besides, he was quite happy with his bachelor status and had no desire to get caught in the parson's mousetrap just yet.

Lipking came into the room bearing more books. "These are from the past three years, my lord."

"No."

"I am sorry, my lord?" Lipking said. He had been about to put the books down on a corner of the desk but stopped with the books in midair.

"I said no, Lipking. I am not going to look at any more books. My neck is aching me, and after having examined the books for the first seven years, I can see that Mr. Straight has been perfectly honest in his handling of the estate's finances."

"Ah. Well, then perhaps you will wish to see these tomorrow?"

"You are not understanding me, Lipking. I trust Straight. You may examine those

61

books if you wish, but I will not."

Lipking looked distinctly crestfallen. "I am simply trying to ensure . . ."

"I know what you are doing, Lipking. It is all that is admirable. And I understand the necessity of examining the entire estate from top to bottom. I, too, want to return the property in perfect order, but I cannot do everything at once." Reath stood up and stretched his legs by walking to the shelf with the wine decanter and poured himself a drink. "Already, I have wasted nearly an entire week here."

"I would not call the time you have spent a waste, my lord. A lot of very necessary work has been done."

"Yes. I suppose so, but that doesn't change the fact that I should have been in London trying to get in contact with Lady Darlington."

"Yes, my lord."

"I will leave first thing tomorrow morning. With luck and my father's excellent horses, I should arrive in town by afternoon. If there is more business you wish for me to attend to here, it will have to wait until I can return."

"Yes, my lord."

Reath looked over at Lipking, who wore a distinctly crestfallen look on his face.

Reath couldn't help but laugh. He walked back and slapped the little man on the back in a friendly way. "Don't look so downcast, Lipking. I promise to return as soon as possible."

"Oh, yes, my lord. I am sure that you will. But I, like you, would like to get this business done and over with."

Sara was too excited. She wanted to see London now, today. She and her aunt had arrived at Langton House the evening before, but her aunt was refusing to stir from her room until noon.

"I am sorry, my dear, but it is simply not done in town," she had said from her bed.

Sara watched, helplessly, as her aunt slowly nibbled at her piece of toast and looked through the enormous stack of invitations which rested beside her on the bed. There had been so many that they had toppled off her tray almost as soon as the maid had set it down. Now Lady Darlington was happily making piles all around her — one to respond favorably to, one to send regrets (this was the smallest pile), and one that she had yet to decide upon.

"How could you possibly get so many invitations so quickly, Aunt?" Sara asked, unable to contain her curiosity.

Lady Darlington looked up, a quizzical smile brightening her face. "Why would I not? I have let it be known that I am bringing a young lady to make her come out. I imagine there are quite a few people who are wondering who this mysterious Miss Whately is." A frown marred her beautiful face. "Actually, I have not yet figured out just how we are going to establish you. I had meant to ask Alston to think of something."

"What do you mean?" Sara asked.

"Well, people will want to know who you are. How confusing it is that my brother took his wife's name when they moved to America, instead of her taking his. I simply do not know how to explain it."

"Then do not. Must we explain our relationship at all?"

"Oh yes. Why, your lineage is extremely important when you want to marry. Any young man's family will want to know — no, demand to know — who your family is. Lineage is *everything*."

"Well, why don't we just say nothing — or say that we are cousins and leave any explanations for later when the need arises?"

"Yes," her aunt said hesitantly, trying to think this through. "Yes, I suppose that is what we will have to do until Alston can think of something better."

Lady Darlington went back to sorting her invitations with a clear conscience, while Sara watched silently. After a moment, Lady Darlington looked up once again at her niece. "Is there something else, Sara?"

"May I go out — just for a walk?"

"Oh no, my dear, not now. We shall go out shopping for your wardrobe later this afternoon, I promise," her aunt reassured her.

Sara frowned, but knew that she had no other choice. Her father had told her again and again that she was to ask her aunt's permission for everything and not to argue with her. It was going to be very difficult to keep her promise. She was simply too used to being her own mistress to sit docilely at home until her aunt was ready to take her out.

Leaving her aunt's room, she wandered aimlessly through the house. She had been up since seven, as was her habit, and had had difficulty keeping herself busy. She had written her father a long letter detailing her adventures so far, with the exception of her excursion to Wyncort — she was not sure he would appreciate her trespassing on what was now someone else's property. She had also followed her natural inclination to try to manage the household, but did not want to look like she was going around her aunt's authority, so she had simply asked the cook if her aunt had given him instructions for the menu for the week. The imperious French chef her aunt kept in London had looked so affronted at her audacity that Sara quickly decided to abandon her idea to help in that direction. Finally, from absolute boredom, Sara had started a sewing sampler from a pattern she had found in a magazine in her aunt's drawing room.

She wished she had been allowed to bring her aunt's horse so that she could go out riding. She had grown very fond of the morning rides she had been able to take each day at Darlington.

Tomorrow, she assured herself, she would see to renting a hack to ride about town. But she needed her aunt's permission to do that as well.

She sat down in the drawing room once again with her sewing. Jabbing her needle into the material in frustration, she managed to pierce it straight into her finger.

It was not until two o'clock that her aunt

declared herself ready to venture out. Sara was so grateful to get out of the house that she nearly ran to their waiting carriage.

"Really, Sara, do please try to behave with a little more decorum," her aunt reprimanded her gently.

They drove the few blocks to Piccadilly, where her aunt's modiste had a small shop. Sara thought it rather odd to drive such a short distance when she and her aunt could have walked it with ease, but she kept her thoughts to herself.

"My young cousin will need a complete wardrobe. Everything from top to bottom, inside and out," Lady Darlington announced, much to the surprise of both Sara and the modiste.

"But I thought I was simply going to get one or two dresses, Aunt Deanna," Sara protested.

"No, no, that would never do. I have seen your wardrobe, such as it is, and you will need everything new. I can't imagine what your father must have been thinking to allow you to go about in such clothes."

Madame Dupres, as the modiste called herself, was naturally thrilled, and had begun walking around Sara examining her size and coloring. "Eet weel be my plaisure, Lady Darlington, my plaisure," she said in her obviously fake French accent. "Zuch a beeootiful young lady. Zuch air! Zuch skin! Just like er beeootiful cousin, non?"

The two older ladies then moved to a worktable, which was quickly covered with bolts of fabric and scattered with fashion plates and sketches.

Sara watched and listened for a short while, but since she was not consulted on any of the decisions, she quickly grew bored. Her frustration from earlier in the day returned in full force. But this time, Sara decided to do something about it — with or without her aunt's permission.

Unnoticed by anyone, Sara quietly left the shop to look in the window of the bookstore a few doors away. It was a completely harmless activity and she was sure she would return before her aunt even noticed she was gone. But a tour guide of the great homes of England, displayed in the window, distracted her and led her mind to thinking about Wyncort.

She had to find a way into that house, she thought as she began to walk again. Now that she was in London, miles away, it was even more difficult. The only thing was to try to return to Darlington, but how? What if she pretended to fall ill or . . .

Sara felt a shiver go down her back. Someone was watching her. She looked up from her reverie to find herself being inspected by a group of men sitting in the bow window of the building across the street. Her pace slowed as she passed and curiously stared back at the men.

If she had not turned her head just when she did, she would have walked straight into the extremely tall, well-dressed man standing directly in front of her.

Six

Stopping short, she found herself a little more than an inch from a striped satin waistcoat.

The most wonderfully clean, and yet surprisingly familiar spicy masculine scent assailed her as she took a step backward and let her eyes move up slowly. She looked past the diamond neatly settled in an exquisitely tied neckcloth, the starched collar points, the strong chin, and into the smugly smiling face of the dreaded handsome viscount.

The gentleman began to laugh. He was not exactly laughing out loud, but his broad shoulders were shaking and his warm gray eyes were squinted with merriment.

"I do beg your pardon," Sara said, lifting her chin a notch, which was not easy because she already had to look up quite a bit to see his face.

He took a step back and gave her a small bow. "My friend, we seem to be developing quite a habit of running into each other. Why is it that I am not at all surprised to see you here?"

Sara had to force herself not to laugh at his pun, but remembering her anger at his high-handedness the last time they had met, easily schooled her face into a serious mask. "I am not your friend. And I do not know . . ." Sara interrupted herself. The stares from the men across the street had become even more intense, and Sara found it very disconcerting. "Could you please tell me who those very rude men are?" she said, nodding her head in the direction of the bow window.

The gentleman looked across the street, the smile on his face broadening. "That is Beau Brummell and his famous bow window set. I can see he is very interested in you."

"Yes, I can see that as well. But why?"

"Why? Well, there are not many young ladies who venture to walk down St. James Street. You are an oddity."

Sara looked around for the first time. It was true. There were no women on this street. She had been so deeply involved in her thoughts that she had not even noticed that she was no longer on Piccadilly.

"Oh dear, I am afraid that I have gotten lost. I had not intended to come this way, I am sure." Sara was extremely embarrassed. She hated having to ask for help, but now she felt horribly out of place and not a little nervous.

She looked up at the man in front of her and the muscles in her stomach tightened.

He had stopped laughing and now, despite the smile still in his eyes, he looked quite concerned — very much as he had when she had been thrown from her horse.

"You are new to town and do not know your way around yet. Where were you meaning to go?" he said kindly.

"I . . . I wasn't meaning to go anywhere, in fact. I mean, not much beyond the bookshop, anyway."

"The bookshop? You mean Hatchards?"

"Yes, that was the name. I was at the modiste's shop with my aunt — er, cousin — and slipped out to look at the books on display in the window, and then I suppose my mind just wandered away, taking me with it." Sara felt her face grow warm. "I assure you, sir, I am not usually such a featherbrain."

The gentleman looked at her quizzically for a moment and she hoped he would not mention the fact that she was riding down the middle of the road the last time they met — another rather silly thing to do. Honestly, she had never behaved this way at home. She could not think of what had gotten into her. She was normally a very practical person.

"You should not abandon your duties so readily, you know," he said with a twinkle in his eye.

"My duties?" Sara was confused for a moment, and then understanding dawned on her and her anger flared. "I am afraid you misunderstand," Sara said, straightening herself and lifting her chin a fraction of an inch. "I have no duties toward my cousin. She is purchasing a wardrobe for me so that I may be presented to the *beau monde*."

"*You* are to have a season?"

"Why, sir, do you sound so surprised?"

The gentleman colored slightly. "I do beg your pardon. I had not thought you . . . If I may I venture to say it, you, Miss, are certain to take the *ton* by storm." He flashed her his beautiful smile.

His eyes then darted back to the gentlemen who were still staring from the bow window. "But not if you stand here any longer." He then quickly took Sara's arm and, turning her around, led her back to Piccadilly.

"Where is the modiste's shop where you left your aunt — er, cousin?" he asked.

Sara blushed again. "She is my cousin,

but I call her aunt." Sara tried to explain and then gave up. She nodded to the shop a little further down the street. "It is there, a few doors down from the bookshop, as I told you."

A lady of some distinction was standing on the street outside of the shop, looking very worried.

"My dear Sara! Where in heaven's name did you wander off to? Oh dear!" the lady cried, the last because she had just caught sight of her cousin's escort.

"Good afternoon, madam." Reath bowed to Sara's cousin, who was unmistakably a lady of the *ton*. "I believe this young lady belongs to you?"

His companion's eyes blazed with anger and she opened her mouth to say something undoubtedly cutting, but was immediately stopped by the lady.

"Yes, indeed. Thank you for returning her safely to me. Lord Reath, is it not?"

Reath was taken aback and wondered who the lady was. She knew him, but he could not for the life of him remember having ever met her before. Was she perhaps some past lover with whom he had had a brief affair?

"Yes, madam. Would you do the honor

of providing an introduction?"

She pursed her lips and then reluctantly said, "Sara Whately, may I present the Viscount Reath?"

Reath bowed. Despite what, if anything, had passed between them, the lady's distant behavior was highly unusual. For a lady to not want to introduce her charge to an eligible *partí* such as himself — notwithstanding his reputation — was extremely odd.

"Miss Whately, your servant." He then turned to her cousin. "Madam, may I suggest that you keep a closer eye on your charge? I am afraid that I met Miss Whately just now walking down St. James Street."

"What!" The lady's face paled considerably and she reached out to Miss Whately, who held on to her with a steady hand while looking daggers at Reath.

"Sara, tell me it isn't so!"

"I am afraid that it is," Sara said. "And there were the rudest men imaginable staring at me from the window of some building."

"That would be White's," Reath put in helpfully.

The lady gave another little moan and leaned more heavily on Miss Whately.

"Aunt Deanna, I think you had better sit down," Miss Whately said, clearly beginning to feel the strain of her cousin's weight on her arm.

"Indeed, ma'am, may I help you, perhaps back to your modiste's shop or to your carriage?" Reath said, reaching for her other arm.

The lady pulled back as if he were going to hurt her with his touch. "No! No, thank you very much, my lord. You have done enough for us already. My, er, cousin will see to my welfare."

Miss Whately helped the lady back to the modiste's shop as Reath stood there helpless and perplexed. He could not understand the aversion the lady had to him, and could only hope that other ladies of the *ton* would not behave in the same way. If he was to find Lady Darlington, he would need the help of such women. Unless . . .

Yes, of course! Either Fungy or Merry was bound to know where to find Lady Darlington. They were active members of the *ton* and had been for the past ten years. They would certainly know everyone who was anyone — and apparently Lady Darlington was a somebody.

Reath turned on his heel and continued

on to White's. He had been heading there when he had run into Miss Whately — again. A small laugh escaped Reath as he turned back down St. James. He really must stop running into her He had to admit, though, each time he did he was more and more intrigued by the plucky young woman.

Sara followed her aunt into the drawing room after they returned from their shopping. Very much like her aunt's favorite drawing room at Darlington, the room was yellow, but the furniture here was much more fashionable and arranged not quite so haphazardly. Blue brocade-covered chairs and sofas in the classic Greek style with curled backs and feet faced each other and sat close to the fireplace.

Sara had been rather surprised that her aunt had said nothing to her once they had reentered the modiste's shop. She had not been sure what to expect, but at least a mild scolding seemed in order if what she had done was in fact as horrible as her aunt's reaction to it seemed to indicate. But her aunt had said nothing, just seen to it that Sara was measured and draped with this fabric and that to see which colors suited her better.

Sara had felt awful. Not only was her aunt spending more money on her than Sara had probably seen in all the past five years together, but she was not even scolding her when she should have been. Sara quickly realized, however, that her aunt's silence on the matter was worse than any scolding she could have received.

What must she think of her? How angry she must be to not even scold her. Waves of guilt for doing something she knew she should not have rolled through her. Would she be sent packing back to her father? No, her aunt was still busy purchasing her wardrobe. Would she be locked in her room? Fed nothing but bread and water? Sara had never been punished before. She had no idea what a punishment might entail.

Sara was now completely miserable and quite repentant. She stayed near the door just inside the drawing room, not sure what to do with herself as Aunt Deanna sped toward Lord Alston, who had been waiting for their return.

"Alston, I can always count on you to be right where I need you," Lady Darlington said as she came into the room. She held out both of her hands to her good friend, who took them warmly in his own.

Looking into her eyes, he said, "Something is amiss. But wait. Before you tell me, I have come with important news I just learned at my club that you should know." He paused, then guided Lady Darlington into a chair before continuing. "Reath is expected in London any day now."

"No, he is already here. We just met him on Piccadilly."

Alston sat down abruptly in the chair opposite to hers. "What happened?"

"I do not believe he knew me, but he asked to be introduced to Sara."

"Oh dear!"

"But that is not the worst of it. Justin, he had just escorted Sara from in front of White's and before the very eyes of Beau Brummell!" Aunt Deanna dropped her head into her hands. "Oh Justin, I am such a terrible chaperon! I did not even notice that Sara had left the modiste's shop. When I stepped outside to see where she had gone, there was Lord Reath escorting her back to me and demanding an introduction."

"Now, now, my dear. It is not your fault." He patted her shoulder. "Miss Whately should have known not to leave you and go wandering off on her own." He frowned at Sara, who suddenly wished the floor would open up and swallow her whole.

Perhaps he saw her remorse, because he then relented and gave Sara a fleeting smile. "And perhaps now Miss Whately knows that it is quite improper for a lady of quality to wander down St. James Street where the gentlemen have their clubs."

She should have indeed known better to not go off by herself. Her aunt had warned her that she was not to go out without someone with her, even a maid or a footman. But she had not thought to go far. It was purely accidental that she had done so. And, of course, she had not known about the peculiar conventions governing St. James Street. She tried to explain as much to her aunt and Lord Alston.

"It is no use, Miss Whately. Unless something can be done, and I do not quite see what, you may have completely ruined your reputation before even attending your first party," Lord Alston said sadly.

"But that is not fair. I did not do it intentionally! As Lord Reath said, I do not know my way about London. I could not know that what I was doing was wrong."

"That does not matter, my dear. This is not about what is fair. This is about what people will say about you and your aunt. And unless something is done, what they say will not be kind."

Seven

At the door of White's, Reath paused and wondered if he could avoid Beau Brummell on his way in. He wanted to avoid the questions he was sure to get from him and his set.

Reath realized that, for some reason, he was extremely loath to discuss Miss Whately with the leader of society — or with anyone else, for that matter. He knew that it would likely lead to her being spoken about in a less than respectful way, and he did not want to see any more harm come to her as a result of her absent-mindedness than was necessary.

He could not understand his sudden feelings of protectiveness for this woman who had been so rude and abrasive toward him each time they had met. Perhaps it was her delicate beauty that brought out the knight-errant in him. Or perhaps it was that he still remembered how she had stood up to him in Portsmouth and how brave she had been when he had nearly run her down. A woman who was so strong and not afraid to speak her mind was an entirely new concept to Reath, and he would not stand for any disrespect toward her. And he certainly was not going to allow her reputation to get soiled within these walls.

Nevertheless, Reath found that he was not entirely able to avoid the questions. No sooner had he entered the reading room, but he was hailed by Lord Alvanley, who had been sitting next to Brummell watching Miss Whately with as much avid curiosity as every other man.

"Ah, here is the man who dares to escort a female down St. James!" Lord Alvanley announced, loud enough for everyone in the room to hear.

A scattering of applause, laughs, and not a few rude remarks were offered by many of the gentlemen sitting nearby.

"This is indeed a warm welcome for your returned comrade," Reath said, good-naturedly. He made his best leg to the assemblage, bowing low.

The appreciation, as well as general remarks of welcome, continued as he began to walk through the room. Luckily, it was not nearly as crowded as it would have been had it been evening, but still there were a good number of gentlemen present.

"My Lord Reath, you must tell us all

who your lovely companion was," Lord Sefton called loudly after him.

Reath stopped. "It was merely a young lady, new to London, who had lost her way," he answered shortly, nodding in his direction.

"But surely you got her name?" his lordship persisted.

"Indeed, my lord, but I would not be much of a gentleman if I was to bandy her name about in such surrounds, now would I?"

"If I recall correctly, you used to be quite generous with the names of your many *chère amie*."

General supporting comments to the same effect echoed from the other gentlemen seated nearby, all listening in on the conversation without shame.

Reath chuckled. "Indeed, but as I said, this was a young lady who had simply lost her way."

"Not a light skirt?"

"No," Reath said, firmly.

"And her chaperon?" Sefton asked, doubtfully.

"I am pleased to say that I was able to return her to the lady unharmed, and I was assured that, in the future, she would keep a closer eye on her charge."

"Going to set up your harem again, Reath?" Lord Chester asked.

Reath laughed to mask the embarrassment he felt at his past foibles being remembered so publicly. "No, I am happy to say I am past that."

"Past having a mistress?" Chester was incredulous.

"Ah, we see a man in his dotage!" another fellow called out amid the laughter.

"It is indeed a sad day when a Reath does not have at least one mistress, if not four!" another said.

"Like father, like son," Chester added. A number of men laughed and chorused their agreement.

"No, no, gentlemen, this is not a laughing matter," Lord Sefton said very seriously. "Clearly our friend Reath has decided that it is high time he settled down and became an obedient stud for some lucky little filly."

Roars of laughter rolled through the room.

When the laughter had mostly died down, Reath said, "You are much too generous, my Lord Sefton. I do not know that I could find a filly who would have one such as I."

"Oh come now, Reath, just wait until the

matchmaking mamas hear that you are available and inclined. You will be besieged."

"I have a sister!" called out a gentleman sitting off to Reath's right.

"And desperate he is to get rid of her!" said his companion.

There was more laughter.

Reath bowed again. "I thank you for your kindness, but alas, I am not quite ready to settle down to that role just yet. Now if you gentlemen will excuse me, there are some friends I have not seen in some time." He bowed once again and moved quickly toward the card room.

His two best friends from school were sitting at a table playing a hand of whist. Not only was he delighted to see his friends here, but he was immediately intrigued by the third making up the table.

A gentleman of Indian ancestry sat holding a fan of cards in his hand and looking very much as if he belonged there. Reath had seen a number of Indians who dressed in Western clothing and copied the Englishmen who came to their cities, but he had never heard of one of them actually coming to England. And even more startling, being allowed entry into a gentleman's club.

"Good afternoon, gentlemen," Reath said as he approached the table.

"Sin!" Fungy and Merry said in unison. His two closest friends, the Honorable St. John Fotheringay-Phipps and Richard Angles, the Marquis of Merrick, both dropped their cards and stood up to give him hearty handshakes and pats on the back.

"Heard you were coming to town," Fungy said.

"We were wondering just when you'd have the nerve to show up here," Merry said at the same time.

Reath couldn't help laughing at his old friends. They were always finishing each other's thoughts.

The three of them had been well known for being inseparable, insufferable, and, to some, indistinguishable. The three of them had done everything together. Each tall and athletic, they had been well known as avid sportsmen, neck-or-nothing riders, and bang up to the mark by their peers. There wasn't a scheme, game, or trick that they hadn't been involved with in some way. And the three of them had hit London like a storm after they had come down from university. After two years of living life to the fullest and engaging in every pursuit open to a young man, Reath had had enough and had gone on to try to do something productive with his life. But the other two had stayed.

Reath looked at his friends. "The years have been good to you." They looked older, but that was to be expected after ten years. He was sure he did as well. No longer were they the fresh-faced youths they had been — now they were men.

First cousins, Fungy and Merry were as tall as he was, both with blond hair, although Fungy's had grown darker and could possibly pass as brown now. They had the same deep green eyes, but Merry always seemed to have a smile on his face, while Fungy had adopted the mannerisms of the dandy and just looked bored. It was also clear to see that Merry had maintained his sportsmanship, while Fungy, although as thin as ever, was clearly no longer the Corinthian but had dissolved into a typical pink of the *ton*.

"You look the same as ever, Sin," Merry said.

"Come play a hand with us," Fungy added, pulling out the fourth empty chair at their table.

Reath held up his hand. "No, I don't play any more. I will happily join you with a bottle of brandy, however." He turned and signaled to a footman.

"Don't play . . ." Fungy began.

Merry burst out laughing. "Haven't lost that sense of humor, Sin!"

Reath smiled. "No, honestly. I haven't played cards in about eight years."

Fungy's mouth nearly dropped open and Merry lost his smile for a moment.

"Very well. Let's sit over by the fire, in that case. But first let me introduce you to our good friend, Julian Ritchie, the Earl of Huntley."

The Indian gentleman stood up and held out his hand. After ten years of living in India, however, Reath had learned Indian ways. He put his hands together in front of his chest, and bowing slightly he said, *"Namaste."*

The man dropped his hand and gave a little grin. "How do you do?"

"Aap se mil kar bahut khush hoon," Reath said smoothly.

The earl raised his eyebrows. "I am afraid I do not speak Hindustani," he responded in his perfect English accent.

"I am terribly sorry. Are you not from India?"

"I am. But I am from Calcutta, where we speak Bengali. I don't suppose you had a chance to see the whole of India?"

Reath laughed, "No, I'm afraid I spent all my time in Lucknow and Delhi. I was fortunate enough to visit Calcutta once or twice, but only for a brief time. I was not there long enough to learn the native language."

Huntley nodded. "There are far too many languages in India for one man to learn, no matter how long he stays there or how widely he travels."

Reath could tell immediately that he was going to like this odd Indian lord. He was eager to learn his story, but first he needed to catch up with his old friends Fungy and Merry.

As they settled into their seats by the fire, Reath poured the brandy for all four of them. And in no time at all, he was hearing all about Merry's latest exploits among the ladies and the demimonde, and Fungy's latest innovations in fashion.

"Are you and Brummell still on speaking terms, then?" Reath asked, his lips twitching with a laugh he was attempting to hold back.

"Wouldn't be fool enough to offend Brummell. And he has wisely adopted my new style in waistcoats." Fungy took a sip of his brandy. "I allow him to claim to have thought of it first, but really it was I whom he saw at Weston's having one made in precisely this style. Recognized the beauty of it, naturally, and had one made for himself. Offered to pay more than I did and managed to get his done first so that it looked like I copied him, rather than the other way round."

"It is indeed a sight to behold, Fungy, especially paired with that neckcloth," Reath said, now beginning to lose his battle with his laughter. He did manage to stop to admire the white and green striped waistcoat and green neckcloth his friend wore. Coupled with the green coat of superfine and pale yellow pantaloons, Reath supposed that he looked complete to a shade.

A look shared with Merry made him completely lose his hard-won composure. Luckily, Fungy took his laughter in stride.

Once he could manage it, Reath said, "You have always been more interested in fashion than anything else, but I can see that you have raised your interest to an art form."

Fungy preened. "Why thank you, Sin. I am glad that someone, besides Julian, appreciates my talent." He leaned forward towards Reath. "Julian, by the way, is entirely my creation."

"Oh?"

"Yes. By gad, should have seen what the boy was wearing when he first arrived here. Took him to my tailor and we got him all straightened out."

Huntley's bright smile of perfectly straight white teeth stood out against the pale brown of his skin. "I shall forever be in your debt, Fungy."

"Nothing," Fungy said, with a wave of his hand.

"I am loath to change to subject, but I had a most interesting encounter on my way here this afternoon," Reath said. "Have any of you heard of a Miss Sara Whately?"

"Whately? I believe I heard that Lady Darlington is sponsoring a girl by that name," Fungy replied.

"Lady Darlington? You don't say," Reath added quickly in a nonchalant manner. He quickly finished off his drink and poured himself another.

"Isn't Lady Darlington the daughter of the fellow you won that estate from just before you left for India? What was his name?" Merry asked.

"Wynsham. How did you know she was his daughter?"

He shrugged. "My mother knows her. I remember Mama saying how upset Lady Darlington was when her father lost their only estate to you. Then, of course, there was all that unpleasantness — well, no need to rehash that, is there?" He paused, looking a little embarrassed.

"Where did you say you met Miss Whately? Haven't even been to one party yet," Fungy asked, obviously impressed.

"I have had the honor of meeting her on no less than three separate occasions since I've returned. But most recently, I met her this afternoon on my way here. She had left her cousin buying her wardrobe at her modiste's shop and accidentally wandered down St. James Street." He paused for a moment. "She has recently arrived from America and does not yet know her way around."

Fungy looked appropriately shocked, Huntley only slightly so, and Merry had begun to laugh.

"I escorted her back to her cousin, who very reluctantly introduced us." Reath paused and took another sip of his brandy. Then half to himself he added, "If that was Lady Darlington, then it solves the mystery of why she was so averse to performing the introduction."

"Oh yes, I cannot imagine that Lady Darlington would be particularly happy to meet you," Merry said. "But what about the girl?"

"She clearly does not know anything."

"Better to keep it that way," Fungy said.

"I am sure that the gossips will be all too happy to inform her of my background," Reath said, frowning into his glass.

"Not if you appear to be accepted by Lady Darlington," Fungy said, thoughtfully.

Reath quirked an eyebrow at him.

Merry sat up. "Yes, of course!"

"What plan are you two hatching?" Reath asked warily.

"Why, nothing yet, but we will think of something momentarily," Merry said with a huge grin on his face.

"You do not want this Miss Whately to know your past history?" Huntley asked, finally rejoining the conversation.

"No, of course not. I am trying to get away from that. I had thought to make a new start."

"Just what I thought," Fungy nodded approvingly.

"And did you not just say that you met Miss Whately walking down St. James?" Huntley said, continuing his thought despite the interruption.

"Yes, why?"

"Well, I know nothing of your past history, but I have learned something of the ways of the *ton* since I've come to England."

"Yes?" the three men said, urging him to continue, as he was clearly on to something.

"It seems to me that people are judged not only by what they have done, but who they are with. When I first came to England, I never would have been accepted into society had Fungy and Merry not supported me. My aunt, Lady Bradmore, was also essential, for she is a respected lady of the *ton*." Huntley stopped and took a sip of his brandy.

"What are you getting at, Julian?" Fungy asked.

"Well, only that if you do not want society filling Miss Whately's ears with tales of your past exploits, then wouldn't it make sense for you to be in her company at a major social event? If she is with you, then the gossips cannot talk to her about you. Also, this way, she will have the advantage of your protection from any negative repercussions her little jaunt down St. James would have had. And you certainly would not be escorting Miss Whately without the approval of her chaperon, Lady Darlington. If Lady Darlington approves of you, there is not much the gossips can say about your past dealings with her family."

Huntley sat back smiling at the stunned faces surrounding him.

"So simple," Fungy said in awe.

"That is the beauty of it," Merry agreed.

"That would indeed solve all of my problems. Do you really think it would work?" Reath asked skeptically.

"Of course it will work," Fungy scoffed.

"Thursday is Lady Bantam's ball. That is your opportunity," Merry said.

"Lady Darlington will never agree to it," Reath said, shaking his head.

"Then don't ask her," said Fungy.

"What? Then how am I going to be Miss Whately's escort for the evening."

Merry nodded. "Ask Miss Whately."

"And how am I to do that without the presence of her cousin?"

"Really, Reath. Been away too long," Fungy sighed.

"Lady Darlington is not going to be at home all the time. She is bound to go out to make social calls. She cannot take Miss Whately with her until the girl has a proper wardrobe. You said yourself that Lady Darlington was purchasing one for her when you met her today. Therefore, Miss Whately is not going to be going out for a few days at least," Merry explained patiently.

"Just go when Lady Darlington is not there. Miss Whately does not know that she should not accept invitations from you, and once the invitation is accepted, it cannot be spurned," Huntley finished.

Reath shook his head. "You all are a devious lot," he said, smiling.

Sara wondered if she could be any more bored. The cook and the housekeeper both had their orders and ran the house with such efficiency that she found that she did not need to give them any direction. Her aunt had gone out to pay morning calls and to try and head off any gossip caused by Sara's walk down St. James Street. And Sara was trapped inside the house, awaiting the first of her new dresses so that she might go out as well.

Coddles came into the room. "Miss Whately, a gentleman is here to see you," he said, very disapprovingly.

Sara stood. She could not imagine which gentleman would be calling on her, especially since she did not know anyone. Still, any sort of diversion was welcome. "Very well, Coddles. Send for Annie to join me and then escort the gentleman up."

Coddles left to do as he was told and within a few minutes returned. "The Viscount Reath," he intoned.

And much to Sara's shock, there he was — the gentleman she had met in three very unfortunate encounters. She quickly determined that this encounter, at least, would go better.

Plastering a smile on to her face, she stepped forward. Holding out her hand, she said, "Lord Reath, what a pleasant surprise." But instead of shaking her hand, as she had expected, Lord Reath bowed and pressed his lips to the back of it. Sara's breath caught in her throat.

"Miss Whately, I am happy to see that your little mishap yesterday has not had any lasting ill effects," he said, smiling warmly at her.

Sara felt her heart begin to beat a little faster. "No, no, indeed, how could it?"

Reath gave a little shrug. "Your cousin did not scold you too badly, I hope?"

She sat down and gestured for Reath to do the same. "No, I am very fortunate, I believe, for having such an understanding relative. She is out, even now, trying to undo some of the damage from my mistake."

"Ah, and that is why I have come to call, as well."

"Oh?"

"Yes. I have come to ask if you might allow me to escort you and your cousin to Lady Bantam's ball tomorrow night."

"I do not know if my cousin was planning on attending or not," Sara answered honestly. "And how would your escort help stop people from talking about me?"

"Well, I have been thinking about it, and I believe that the easiest way to stop the gossip about you and your cousin would be for the two of you to be seen in my company. It was I, after all, whom you met in front of White's. If Beau Brummell and his cronies see that you and I are friends, then they will be less likely to think the worst of you."

"And my cousin will be spared any negative talk as well?"

"Absolutely."

Sara thought about this. She had been so anxious after what Lord Alston had said to her about how people would gossip. And it was not so much her own reputation that she was worried about, for she honestly cared very little for that, but rather, for what people would say about her aunt.

Society was so very important to Lady Darlington — indeed, it was her life. Sara would have been much more upset had there been any lasting effects to her aunt's reputation. But if Lord Reath escorted them to this ball, then everyone would see that they were in each other's good graces. And surely, as Lord Reath said, that would stop any gossip.

"Thank you, sir. I would be happy to accept your invitation," Sara replied, making a quick decision.

Reath looked pleased, his devastating smile spread across his face. He was truly quite amazingly handsome when he smiled.

Standing and then bowing low over Sara's hand once again, he said, "I look forward to seeing you tomorrow night then. I shall come by around nine to pick up both you and your cousin."

Sara could not help but return his smile.

Her aunt came in not long after Lord Reath left.

"Aunt Deanna, the most wonderful thing," Sara said, jumping up from the sofa where she had once again been trying to entertain herself with her embroidery.

Her aunt stopped and gave her niece a bright smile of anticipation.

"Lord Reath was here and he has offered to escort us to Lady Bantam's ball tomorrow night. It will solve all of the problems caused by my mistake."

Lady Darlington blanched. Quickly, Sara led her aunt to the sofa and began to fan her. "What is it, Aunt Deanna? He assured me that if we were seen in his company that society would not gossip any more about my meeting him on St. James Street."

"Oh Sara," her aunt wailed. "You did not accept?"

"But of course I did. I do so want to make amends for what I have done — and he assured me that this would do just that."

"Oh, my dear. No, you could not know. Such an innocent." Her aunt gently patted Sara's cheek, but looked like she was about to cry. "There is nothing to be done, I suppose. Now we must go through with it."

Her aunt was talking in riddles. What was it about Lord Reath that upset her aunt so? He was clearly a gentleman and had been very kind to her the past two times they had met. Sara could not imagine what her aunt had against the man, and her aunt was clearly not going to explain it.

Eight

Reath was exceedingly pleased with the way his friends' plan had worked. The evening, he hoped, would be an exceptional one. Now he would finally be able to rectify not only the horrible mistake he had made in his youth, but cleanse his past reputation as well.

With Lady Darlington's outward acceptance of him, the other high sticklers of the *ton* would have no choice but to also accept him. He would be in Lady Darlington's company for much of the evening and surely would get a chance to ask her for her brother Lord Wynsham's direction. And, as an added bonus to all this, he would be with the lovely Miss Whately. He hoped she would be as pleasant as she was on their last meeting, rather than rude as she had been during their first few meetings. Reath could barely keep from rubbing his hands together in anticipation.

He had not been altogether surprised that, when he presented himself at Langton House, Lady Darlington had been pale and clearly not well pleased with his escort. What had been rather more surprising, however, was Miss Whately.

He had believed Miss Whately to be striking when he had met her in Portsmouth. Then she had been dressed in her dowdy round traveling dress. He had thought her to be appealing even when covered in dirt after being thrown from her horse. And she had been delightful when he had met her on St. James Street, even dressed in her outmoded cloak and bonnet. But when he saw her that evening dressed in a fashionable evening gown, with her chestnut curls framing her sweet face, he forgot to breathe for a few minutes. She was incredibly beautiful.

Her white dress complimented her creamy complexion, and the blue overdress highlighted her large and engaging blue eyes. Her soft hair was pulled up in a complicated braid which wound around her head. And she had the same enticing smell of roses and lemons about her, which teased at his senses whenever he leaned close. She looked the picture of delicate feminine innocence, but with a flash of spirit that was all her own.

He managed to restrain himself so that he only lightly kissed the back of her hand when they met, but it was her beautiful pink lips that looked ready to be kissed. He stifled an overwhelming desire to pull off his gloves and touch the swell of creamy flesh that looked so enticing above the low neckline of her dress.

But he did not. He behaved as the model English gentleman.

As they left Lady Darlington's home and again as they entered Lady Bantam's ball room, he was surprised to realize just how good, how right, she felt on his arm. It was as if they were meant to be together. Reath quickly shook such fancies from his mind and concentrated on the evening to come.

"Oh my, oh my, oh my! Good evening, Lady Darlington. Lord Reath, what an honor it is to have you grace my little gathering," Lady Bantam said, sweeping her hand to indicate the already overcrowded room.

"Good evening, Lady Bantam." Reath bowed.

"May I present my cousin, Miss Sara Whately?" Lady Darlington said, an awkward smile plastered on to her face.

As Miss Whately curtsied, Reath wondered if she too was as nervous as Lady Darlington clearly was — or perhaps she was simply overwhelmed by her first introduction into society. She was being uncharacteristically quiet, and her smile was even less believable than her cousin's. Miss Whately's eyes darted here and there as she took in the magnificence of the ball.

Lady Bantam tittered. "I hear that you are determined to make a name for yourself even before you have been presented, Miss Whately."

Miss Whately's eyes snapped back to Lady Bantam, and Lady Darlington began to turn bright red.

Reath distracted Lady Bantam's attention by laughing loudly. "Indeed, Lady Bantam. Poor Miss Whately inadvertently had a *complete* tour of Mayfair the other afternoon."

Lady Darlington, too, forced out a laugh. "Lud, what a lark that was! The poor dear got totally turned around after looking in the window of Hatchards, and made a wrong turn while she was returning to meet me at the modiste's shop. And the funniest thing was that I was right next door at Madame Dupres's." She leaned closer to their hostess and said, confidentially, "It is her first time in London, you know."

Lady Bantam gave Miss Whately a sympathetic look, while the young lady herself suddenly found the floor very interesting.

"And you, my lord, are the hero in this farce, I understand," Lady Bantam said, fluttering her eyelashes in his direction.

"Oh, I can hardly call myself a hero, but I was happy to be of service to Miss Whately," he said, noticing that Miss Whately's hands were clasped tightly in front of her. She was clearly battling to keep her tongue in check.

"Well, she is certainly a very lucky young lady to be rescued by such a handsome, eligible man — and a viscount no less," Lady Bantam gushed.

Miss Whately's eyes focused once more on Lady Bantam as she lost the battle within herself. "Surely, ma'am, his title has no bearing on the matter. The point is that he is a friend and was kind enough to help me find my way back to my cousin, is it not?"

"Well, yes, I suppose," Lady Bantam's smile had become more forced, "but it is so much more pleasant that he is a viscount. He lends more countenance to you, and society is more likely to forgive you your mistake since Lord Reath sees no harm in it. Is that not so, Lady Darlington?"

"Indeed, Lady Bantam. I have been trying to explain as much to Sara, but she is from America and does not understand," Lady Darlington said, shaking her head sadly.

"But I . . ." Miss Whately began.

"Yes, of course. Lady Bantam, would you be so kind as to excuse us? I see some friends of mine I have promised to introduce to Miss Whately." Reath deftly bowed to Lady Bantam while taking Miss Whately's arm and leading her and her cousin away.

A glance in Miss Whatley's direction made Reath nearly laugh out loud. She had pressed her lips together in an attempt to keep her rude retort from popping out. Reath silently applauded her attempts at good behavior and hoped that she would be able to keep it up for the rest of the evening.

Lady Darlington greeted the many avid stares of her acquaintances with an appropriate glare as they passed through the crowd as quickly as Reath could manage with decorum.

"That was very well done, my lord. You averted a potentially unpleasant scene," Lady Darlington said quietly to him so that only he could hear.

He smiled down at her. "Yes. I believe I am beginning to get your cousin's measure. She seems to have quite a temper, and a tongue to go with it."

Lady Darlington flushed lightly. "I am afraid so, my lord. It is a typical Whately trait, I am afraid."

"And I must thank you, my lady, for playing along as well," Reath said.

"Yes, well, there was little else I could do." Lady Darlington still did not look very happy, but she at least had not given the game away.

Sara was much too involved in looking about her to pay attention to the whispers of her aunt and Lord Reath. The room they were in was completely packed with glittering people. She had never seen so much finery before in her life. It was rather overwhelming. She felt so small and plain among the beautiful people of the *beau monde*. She knew herself to be looking exceptionally fine, but that did not stop her from feeling nervous.

Lord Reath led the two of them up to two gentlemen who were standing and talking by the far wall. They were similar in height, and both strikingly handsome with dark blond hair. But one was dressed in such a fashion that Sara was tempted to wonder how he could move. His light blue breeches were impossibly tight, his shirt points reached to his cheeks, a blue neck-cloth was tied in an impressive knot around his throat, and his dark blue coat looked as if it had to have been sewn on to him, it fit so perfectly.

Sara felt even smaller and more insignificant next to such magnificence. The other gentleman was dressed very much like Lord Reath, with an understated elegance in black and white.

"Lady Darlington, Miss Whately, may I present my very good friends, Lord Merrick and his cousin, the Honorable Mr. Fotheringay-Phipps."

Lady Darlington inclined her head graciously. "Mr. Fotheringay-Phipps and I have had the pleasure of meeting before. Lord Merrick, it is an honor to meet you."

Sara was almost surprised when there was no ripping sound accompanying Mr. Fotheringay-Phipps's bow as he managed to bend low over her aunt's hand and then her own. Lord Merrick also turned his attention to Sara after properly greeting Lady Darlington.

"We hear you have recently arrived from America, Miss Whately," Lord Merrick said.

"Yes, sir, but a week ago."

"And how do you find our fair isle?" Mr. Fotheringay-Phipps asked.

"Very well. It is quite lush and green, but I have been in the country this past week and only just arrived in London a few days ago."

"And already we have the honor of your presence at this gathering," said Lord Merrick with a quick and easy smile.

"Lord Reath was kind enough to offer to escort us after I, er, got lost. He thought it best if my aunt and I were seen in his company this evening."

"Don't mean to say that you would rather not have been in his company, I am sure," Mr. Fotheringay-Phipps said, raising his eyebrows to Lord Reath.

Lord Reath, too, was staring at her with one eyebrow raised.

"No, of course not, since the whole purpose of being with him is to fix my own mistake," Sara said, shrugging her shoulders with indifference.

Lord Merrick and Mr. Fotheringay-Phipps both turned to look at Lord Reath, who looked nonplussed for a moment. He then laughed and said, "Well, I am honored that you accepted my escort toward that end."

The other gentlemen laughed and Aunt

Deanna turned slightly pink, but Sara did not see what was so funny.

Aunt Deanna was distracted by a friend of hers who pulled her away. Was it possible that she looked relieved? No, she must just be happy to see her friend, Sara thought to herself.

Lord Reath, in turn, moved away to greet a lady who was approaching them.

"You do realize, Miss Whately, that you are currently being envied by most of the young ladies present?" Lord Merrick said.

Sara looked around, and indeed there were quite a number of ladies looking her way. She also could not help but notice that the lady with Lord Reath was standing very close to him and smiling up at him in the most beguiling fashion. Lord Reath, in his turn, seemed to be enjoying the lady's attentions a great deal, for he too was smiling and leaning down toward her. They would have had to be embracing to get any closer, Sara thought with disgust. She tore her attention away and forced her mind back to the conversation at hand.

"Envied? Why is that, sir?"

"Because Lord Reath is a gentleman who is much sought after."

"Extremely eligible. Titled and rich — not to mention not all that bad to look at either," Fungy added.

"Oh." Sara supposed she should be impressed by this, but found that she simply could not muster up any enthusiasm for Lord Reath's title and wealth. As for his looks . . . well, so what if he were by far the most handsome among those present, with his excellently fitting clothes making Sara all too aware of his superb physique?

Clearly, the lady he was speaking with had also noticed how handsome he was. Sara found that she was beginning to get rather annoyed at just how amusing Lord Reath was being as his companion laughed adoringly at something he said. He must certainly be a rake of no short order to be so utterly charming.

She remembered the warm looks he had given her earlier that evening when they had met at her aunt's house. She had never been tongue-tied in her life, but when he looked deep into her eyes as he had kissed the back of her hand, she found that her mind had gone absolutely blank.

But now she thought she understood why he had kissed her hand and looked at her in that way. It was not that he was attracted to her in particular, it was that she was a woman and that was the way he behaved with all women. *Disgusting.*

There was an awkward silence as Sara tried to control her sudden anger. She tried once again to put Lord Reath from her mind and turned back to the gentlemen next to her.

"Mr. Fotheringay-Phipps, have you read the latest offering from Mr. Wordsworth?"

"Mr. Who?" Mr. Fotheringay-Phipps asked, clearly startled.

"Mr. Wordsworth — William Wordsworth."

"He is a poet, is he not?" Lord Merrick asked.

"Yes. Are you not familiar with his work?" Sara asked. She had been sure that everyone in England would know of the great poets who resided within their shores.

"Poetry? No, never touch the stuff." Mr. Fotheringay-Phipps shivered visibly.

Lord Merrick laughed. "Fungy is not one to read anything beyond the gossip columns," he explained.

"You do not read? I have never heard of a gentleman who did not read poetry. Although I must admit, my experience with gentlemen is limited to my father's friends, and they are all poets." A man who did not read — this was an entirely new concept to Sara. "Do you read, Lord Merrick?" Sara asked, turning to that gentleman.

"I have been known to pick up a journal now and again, and I have read Byron's poems, of course."

"Oh, well, you must read Wordsworth, and Coleridge . . ."

"Miss Whately, may I make a suggestion?" Mr. Fotheringay-Phipps interrupted her.

"Yes?"

"Unless you want to be thought a bluestocking, I would not go around asking people if they have read this poet or that."

Sara looked up into his gently smiling face. She could tell that he intended his comment to be some good, kind advice, but she had no idea what he meant. "Please excuse my ignorance, but what is a bluestocking?"

The gentlemen looked startled.

"A bluestocking is a lady who prefers scholarly pursuits rather than social ones," Lord Merrick explained.

"Oh. You say this as if it were something bad," Sara said.

"It is," the two gentlemen said in unison.

Sara did not know what to do. She was completely perplexed. She looked from one man to the other, at a loss as to what to say.

"I . . . I will try to avoid that then," she said. "Thank you for your advice."

But if she couldn't discuss poetry, what could she discuss, Sara wondered. She looked over at her aunt, now speaking with Lord Reath. She did not look particularly happy with her conversation either.

Lord Merrick coughed loudly enough for Lord Reath to hear him and turn around. He looked from his friends to Sara and then excused himself from his conversation with Lady Darlington.

Sara gratefully traded places with him. "Why do you look so upset, Aunt? I do hope that Lord Reath has not said anything to disturb you?"

Her aunt looked startled for a moment, and then forced a smile onto her face. "Oh no! No, not at all, my dear Sara." She paused and then added under her voice, "How very perceptive you are, indeed."

She then brightened up, forcibly. "No, we were merely discussing . . . ah, er, a sad piece of gossip. Some poor girl who quite ruined herself by going off with a young man alone in a closed carriage. It was quite distressing to hear. That is why I was looking upset."

Sara didn't believe her aunt for a moment, but clearly she did not want to tell

Sara about what she and Lord Reath had really been discussing. She could simply have said as much, Sara thought, instead of making up this faradiddle.

Sara turned and, for a few minutes, silently watched the people dancing in the middle of the floor. Shc had never learned how to dance. It looked like fun, with lots of pretty turns and some graceful steps. The dance ended and Sara watched the happy faces of those who had been dancing as they went off to seek refreshment or a breath of fresh air.

A gentleman approached a young lady standing nearby. He bowed as the young lady curtsied. They exchanged a few words and then, with the brightest of smiles, they both went off to join the others who were assembling for the next dance.

"Would you care to dance, Miss Whately?" Lord Reath's quiet voice startled her out of her reverie.

"Oh. I . . . I would be most honored to dance with you, sir," Sara said, copying what she had just heard other the young lady say. She curtsied and then placed her hand on his outstretched arm.

This should not be difficult at all, Sara thought, eagerly. She could simply copy what the other dancers did.

Keeping a close eye on the woman next to her, Sara attempted to do just as she did. Unfortunately, she found by looking around that she was supposed to be doing something slightly different. Not every couple was doing the same thing at the same time. Sara quickly realized that she was supposed to lead the second couple behind them, but she had no idea what she was to do.

Lord Reath looked at her oddly. "No, Miss Whately, it is you who are supposed to turn now," he said gently. Sara turned, but went the wrong way.

"Take his hand first," he said, directing her to the partner of the young lady standing next to her.

And then finally, he began to laugh. "Miss Whately, do you not know how to dance?"

Sara looked at him, completely frustrated. It had all looked so simple! But when actually called upon to do the steps, she just did not know what to do and when.

And now he was laughing at her! Sara swallowed the lump that had suddenly formed in her throat.

Lord Reath took her elbow and directed her back to her aunt. Still laughing, he said, "Miss Whately, you only needed to tell me that you did not dance and I would have been happy with that. You did not need to attempt something of which you have no knowledge."

"Sara, what was that?" her aunt said, pumping her fan vigorously in front of her face.

Sara looked from her aunt to Lord Reath. Looking down at her hands clenched in front of her, she blinked a few times rapidly to clear the tears that had sprung to her eyes.

"I am sorry, sir. It looked so much easier than it actually was. I am afraid I never learned how to dance."

"Nor appropriate conversation, from what Fungy and Merrick tell me," Lord Reath said, nearly laughing at her.

"Whatever do you mean, my lord?" Her aunt was clearly becoming more agitated by the moment.

"Apparently, Miss Whately attempted to speak to Lord Merrick and Mr. Fotheringay-Phipps about some poet or other she has read. Not a wise choice of topics, I'm afraid," he said, directing this last statement to Sara.

"Sara, is this true?" her aunt asked.

"Yes. I did not realize that discussing poetry was inappropriate, but Lord Merrick and Mr. Fotheringay-Phipps were kind enough to point this out to me."

"Oh, my dear! What *did* your father teach you?" Aunt Deanna asked, sounding rather disturbed.

"Why, nothing," Sara said in almost a whisper, her voice suddenly refusing to cooperate.

Lord Reath burst out laughing. "That much is clear."

Sara glared at her escort. She could not see what was so amusing in her mistakes. It was not her fault, nor her father's, that she had had no time for such frivolities. She wished she could say as much, but she knew now was not the time for such confessions. So instead, she bit back her tongue and let her eyes convey her anger and hurt.

Lord Reath seemed to get the message quickly, for he stopped laughing almost immediately.

"No, my dear Miss Whately, you must excuse me, that was not well done. I beg your forgiveness," he said, in the first display of seriousness she had seen from him all evening.

Her anger immediately dissipated. "It is all right, sir. I should not have attempted to dance when I do not know the steps."

"I would be most honored if you would allow me to teach you," he said, bowing to her.

Sara was touched. Not only had he immediately stopped laughing at her, but now he was offering to help her. He was indeed a very kind gentleman. "Thank you, sir. I very much would like to learn."

"Yes, and so you shall. Although your offer was exceedingly gracious, my lord, I am afraid we cannot accept. I will hire a proper dancing instructor for Sara." Her aunt sounded most definite on this matter.

Lord Reath looked at her silently for a moment and then nodded his head. "As you wish, my lady."

"Now, Lord Reath, I will not monopolize you. If you would like to dance with some other young lady present, please feel free to do so," Sara said, as another woman walked past them slowly, trying to catch her escort's eye.

Lord Reath obviously had not seen her, for he looked quizzically at Sara and then bowed and went off in the other direction.

"Oh dear," her Aunt Deanna said as she watched him walk away.

Nine

Once again he had been dismissed by the chit, Reath chuckled to himself. What was it about this girl that she felt she could simply dismiss him out of hand? He had never in his life experienced such treatment from a woman.

Reath did not have long to ponder the odd behavior of Miss Whately, since he was immediately hailed by Lady Patrick.

"My Lord Reath, I do hope that you have not forgotten me?" the titian-haired beauty said, fluttering her eyelashes at him.

Reath could not suppress a broad smile. "How could I ever forget you, Susannah? You are as beautiful as ever," he said smoothly as he lingered over her hand.

"And you are charming as ever," she purred.

"Did I hear correctly? Am I to offer you my condolences?"

The lady looked suitably sad. "Yes. I am afraid my dearest husband departed this world two years ago." She looked up at him from under her eyelashes. "I am a widow — although, as you see, no longer in mourning."

He took in her bright green dress with its shockingly low neckline. Reath wondered how she managed to keep all of her ample bosom from spilling out. Certainly, she had to move carefully to keep that from happening.

"Perhaps you would be willing to stop by my home later this evening?" she said, interrupting his perusal of her person. "I would love to welcome you back — properly." She leaned toward him invitingly, and he did not miss her meaning.

The thought was very enticing. He remembered well the brief liaison they had shared before he left for India. She was a passionate woman, and her aging husband had been incapable of fulfilling her strong desires. Reath had been only too happy to oblige. But oddly enough the thought of such carnal occupations did not appeal to him just at this moment.

The sweet, innocent face of Miss Whately floated in front of his mind's eye. He shook his head to rid himself of any thoughts in that direction. She was not eligible for the sort of entertainments a man would enjoy engaging in, no matter how much he might be attracted to her. He could barely believe that he even thought of engaging in such pursuits with Miss

Whately — and quickly, though reluctantly, he put the idea from his mind.

What did, however, strike him as exceedingly unusual was his behavior that evening. While he was enjoying flirting with the ladies of his acquaintance, he had no desire to go any further than that. He had had a few minutes' conversation earlier with another of his old *chère amie,* earlier and she too had wanted him to visit her. It had taken him a little while to charm her out of the pet she had taken when he had said no. He hoped Susannah would not be as difficult.

"Your offer, my dear, is extremely attractive — nearly as attractive as you," he said to Lady Patrick. "I am afraid, however, that I have a prior engagement for this evening."

"With whom?" she asked, a little peevishly.

Reath chuckled. "I shall not tell you, but be assured, they are not nearly as lovely as you." He kissed the inside of her wrist, giving her a knowing smile.

Lady Patrick shivered with delight. "Perhaps another time then, my lord?"

Reath raised one eyebrow. "Perhaps."

He moved on.

He had intended to circle the room and

make for the card tables, but before he could even get close to the door, he was trapped once again.

This time it was Princess Lieven who approached with a young lady in tow. "My lord, please allow me to present you to Miss Scott."

Reath bowed over the young lady's hand. He had heard of Miss Scott from Merry. She was deemed one of the season's incomparables — and for a very good reason. She was exceptionally pretty. Her white dress was the height of fashion for a young lady, and her dark brown hair was twisted into a complicated knot at the top of her head with perfect ringlets surrounding her face.

But it was her bright green eyes that drew his attention. They looked at him in such a calculating fashion that he wondered whether she was figuring exactly how much he was worth, or just how long it would take to bring him up to scratch.

The orchestra played the introduction to the next set of country dances, and Reath was trapped.

"I am honored to make your acquaintance, Miss Scott. Would you care to dance?"

The young lady curtsied with the perfection of years of practice, unlike the bob that Miss Whately usually gave him. "I would be delighted, my lord."

Leading her out on to the floor, he knew that he would not have the difficulties he had had with Miss Whately. And, indeed, the young lady moved with grace and a certainty that was rather a relief after his last dance.

"You dance beautifully, Miss Scott."

"Thank you, my lord. Might I say the same of you?"

He nodded.

"I imagine it is easier to dance with someone who knows the steps better than your last partner."

"Ah, yes. Poor Miss Whately. I believe she was simply nervous. This is the first ball she has ever been to."

Miss Scott inclined her head and smiled sympathetically.

The young lady said all the right things, not once making any disparaging remarks about his title nor asking inappropriate questions.

Reath was bored beyond belief.

Once he had been seen dancing with Miss Scott, all of the other young ladies out on the prowl that season joined in the hunt. He quickly realized that he did not stand a chance.

As soon as he left the side of one young lady, another was introduced to him.

"Oh, my Lord Reath," one young lady giggled, "I hear you are one of the most eligible gentlemen this season."

Reath felt the noose begin to slip over his head. He must remove it quickly or else he would be sought after in this way the entire season. "I am afraid you are mistaken, Miss Compton. I am not currently looking to marry."

The young lady giggled again. "Oh no, I have never heard of a gentleman who was, and yet they do so all the same."

The knot tightened. Momentarily, his neckcloth felt rather constricting. Reath ran a finger along the inside of his collar. But then he straightened, calling himself to order.

This was nothing new. He knew exactly how to deal with young ladies out for his title and wealth. They were all the same, these proper young ladies. They presented no challenge and nothing surprising. He handled them with aplomb, gently flirting, and then passing them on to the next sorry chap.

He caught a glimpse of Miss Whately talking with Chaddsworth-Hervey. She looked completely bored.

He should try and remember to mention to her that she should at least try to look interested in what a gentleman was saying to her. Knowing Chaddsworth-Hervey, he was probably prosing on about the latest bits of blood he had purchased for his stud farm.

Reath laughed. Forcing such an intelligent and spirited girl to do the pretty at a ball was such a shame, especially when there were so many insipid, well-trained girls to do their part. Secretly, he hoped she would give Chaddsworth-Hervey one of her stinging set-downs. He watched as Miss Whately clasped her hands together in front of her and bit her lip. She was trying so hard to be good. He had to go and rescue her.

"Do you read, Mr. Chaddsworth-Hervey?" Sara asked the gentleman. She desperately had to get him to change the topic before she died of boredom.

Her aunt, standing next to Sara, gave her side a poke with her fan. Sara supposed that to mean that she had just asked something inappropriate.

Mr. Chaddsworth-Hervey smiled condescendingly down at Sara, his yellowed teeth contrasting nicely with his bottle green coat. "Is this how you Americans make a joke?" he asked.

Sara forced a laugh. "Yes. I had hoped you would find it amusing."

Mr. Chaddsworth-Hervey snuffled like a pig and then said, "Yes. Highly amusing."

"The weather has been particularly fine the past few days, has it not?" Sara tried again. No poke from her aunt. This was a good sign.

"Yes, indeed, Miss Whately. We are not quite used to seeing so much sunshine. Do you have it in America?" he asked with all seriousness.

Sara blinked. "Sunshine? Yes, Mr. Chaddsworth-Hervey. We have quite a bit. Naturally, it rains a lot in the springtime, but come summer it is sunny almost every day."

The gentleman seemed to have difficulty understanding this concept. "Sunny almost every day? My, my, how can you stand it?"

"I must admit that I enjoy it, sir."

"Chaddsworth-Hervey," Lord Reath said, strolling up to them.

Sara stifled a sigh of relief.

"Ah, Reath. Heard you were back. You were at White's this afternoon. Heard all about it. Little filly, eh?" He snorted and slapped Lord Reath on the back.

Lord Reath smiled wanly. "I thought you might be interested in something I just overheard — Miss Price-Liste talking about you to her chaperon."

"Eh? You don't say." He sketched a quick bow to the ladies. "You will please excuse me."

"Thank you, sir. That was exceedingly kind of you," Sara said, watching Mr. Chaddsworth-Hervey's quickly retreating back and giving Lord Reath one of her rare smiles.

"It is entirely my pleasure, Miss Whately," he said, smiling back.

A rush of warmth slid into Sara's stomach.

Sara had tried all evening to stop comparing every gentleman to Lord Reath. It was completely unfair, she knew, and she should not do so. But somehow with every gentleman she met, she could not help but think how much shorter he was than Lord Reath, or how narrow his shoulders looked compared to Lord Reath's.

Or, what disconcerted her the most, was how boring these other gentlemen seemed when compared to the odd sense of humor that Lord Reath had. Many of the men she spoke to attempted to make witticisms, but not one of them was actually amusing. At least when Reath attempted to be funny, he usually succeeded.

If only she was at leisure and had an inclination to marry. But she knew that it was up to her to save her family's fortunes. That she had to attend these silly parties to appease her aunt was almost more than she could bear. But to actually be attracted to a gentleman was not something that Sara had planned on, nor had time for.

Sara had also never thought that she would be attracted to a rake. She had always imagined herself with some quiet literary gentleman. But then again, that was the only type of gentleman she had ever met.

It was strange. She felt entirely at her ease in Lord Reath's presence — and yet slightly on edge, as if there should be more for her to do with him than engage in polite conversation. She did not know what, and it made her warm and uncomfortable thinking about it. She did, however, very much like the feeling she had when he was near.

"I do hope that the rest of your evening was enjoyable," Lord Reath said, as he sat back among the squabs of his well-sprung carriage on their way back to her aunt's house.

"Very much, sir, thank you," Sara lied. "And yours?"

"It was well enough. I saw that you were quite as busy with the gentlemen as I with the ladies. I cannot imagine that anyone was rude enough to mention your walk down St. James?"

"No. I believe my exhibition on the dance floor put my first faux pas right out of everyone's mind."

Reath laughed, while her aunt stifled a groan.

"And you did not have too much difficulty making conversation?" he asked.

"No," Sara was pleased to be able to say. "Once I caught on to what was acceptable and what was not, it was quite simple."

"Ah, excellent. Would you care to share your insights with me? I could always use some advice on what to discuss while making the dull rounds of parties."

Sara frowned at him, not believing that he would ever be at a loss of what to discuss nor think that attending parties was dull. He had looked like he was having an excellent time every time Sara had caught a glimpse of him that evening.

But then she shrugged and said, "Well, from Aunt Deanna's generous pokes at me with her fan, I have learned that anything in the least bit intellectual or pertaining to any sort of literature is unacceptable. The current political situation also seems to be inappropriate, but that I understand considering the tensions we've been having between our two countries."

Sara paused for a moment, trying to remember what was appropriate. "I suppose anything that is shallow or insipid is perfectly fine, is that not so, Aunt?"

"Oh well, to be sure, I would not say . . ."

Lord Reath's laughter interrupted whatever her aunt was going to say. "I would say you got it right on the mark, Miss Whately. Touché. I knew that you would see through to our shortcomings immediately."

Lady Darlington sniffed her disapproval loudly. "I am still horrified at how spectacularly ill-prepared you are to be presented to society. I can not imagine how your father had the nerve to raise his only daughter in this shimble-shamble way. And I must offer you my heartfelt apologies, Lord Reath. If I had only realized that it was the case, I never would have allowed you to escort us this evening. Indeed, I would not have allowed, and will not allow, Sara to attend any more social functions until she had been taught the proper way to behave."

There was a pause, and then, from his side of the carriage, Reath said quietly, "If you will permit me, Lady Darlington, I believe that Miss Whately's unique outlook and keen intelligence will allow her to continue in society quite successfully. At the very worst, she will be considered an original, and you know that there is nothing more attractive to many than that."

Sara could feel his eyes boring into her even through the dark. She was happy that there was no light, because she knew that he could not see the grateful tears that had sprung to her eyes as he defended her.

Ten

"Have you no other horses that I could use?" Sara asked the ostler of the stables, looking at the swaybacked animal in front of her.

"This or nothin'," the man answered, spitting on the ground.

"But this is unacceptable. This horse is barely capable of standing on his own legs, let alone carrying a rider. Surely you have another . . ."

"Look, Miss, d'ye want the 'orse or not?" the man interrupted her.

Sara looked the horse over once more. It infuriated her that this man could stand there and lend out this poor old nag for anyone to ride. She dug her hand into her reticule.

Her aunt had finally given her permission to ride, and Sara just could not wait until Lord Alston could rent a hack for her. But she had not imagined that she would have any trouble with such a simple task, nor that such sorry animals were provided. Now, unfortunately, she realized that she had been wrong.

She pulled out a few coins and handed

them over. Her desire to ride was stronger than her pride, and she suspected that it was early enough in the morning that no one of any consequence would see her up on this sad-looking beast.

She was very sadly mistaken. It seemed to be a rather popular time of day to go out riding, and she had the misfortune to pass by quite a number of gentlemen she had met the previous evening. Although she recognized only two of the ladies who were out, their laughter at seeing her on this nag echoed in her ears for a good five minutes after she had nodded her greeting.

Still, she held her head high as she continued around the park. And it was in this pose that she had the extreme misfortune to meet Lord Reath, who was out on the most beautiful chestnut she had ever seen.

As he turned his horse to walk beside hers, she had no choice but to speak to him.

"How do you do, sir?" Sara said, deliberately ignoring his shaking shoulders, which showed that he was laughing at her, even though he was doing an admirable job of not laughing right out loud.

"I am very well, Miss Whately, and yourself?" he managed to say, while desperately trying to keep a straight face.

"Quite fine, thank you." Sara kept her gaze directed in front of her. "It is a lovely day, is it not?"

"Yes. The weather has been unusually pleasant this past week."

There was a pause in their conversation as Sara searched for something else un-exceptional to say.

"Miss Whately, may I be so bold as to ask from where you obtained that . . . that animal you are riding? Surely it is not from your cousin's stables."

Sara gave a little laugh. "I believe you are being very kind, sir, in your choice of words. I am afraid that Lady Darlington did not wish to go to the trouble of sta-bling any more than her carriage horses while in town. I was forced to rent this poor old nag from a stable nearby."

"I see. Perhaps you might allow me to see if there is another horse available from the same stable?"

"I was assured that there were none. And if there were, perhaps they are all in this same sad state."

"Despite what you were told, I think I might be able to persuade the ostler to find a horse in better condition for you to ride."

Sara turned and looked Lord Reath di-rectly in the eye. "I assure you sir, I tried my best to do just that and I was repeatedly told that this was the only horse he had for rent."

"Even so, I see we are nearing the gate, so it will do no harm to simply ride over and see if there aren't any at this time."

Sara could tell that he was not going to give up, so she directed the nag in the direction of the stable. The animal managed to give the impression of some enthusiasm as it headed home.

Lord Reath dismounted at the stable. But when he lifted her down, Sara had the oddest sensation of tingles all through her body. She removed her hands from his broad shoulders as quickly as she could after he placed her gently on the ground, but could not remove her eyes so easily from looking deeply into his.

His eyes were not only the most lovely color of gray she had ever seen, but there was something else, something warm and caring in them, as if he wanted nothing more than to make her happy.

She was saved from embarrassment by the ostler, who came out to greet the well-dressed gentleman. This time he did not spit on the ground even once, but instead bowed in the most respectful way imaginable.

Lord Reath, seeing the ostler approach, gave Sara a smile and a wink. He then turned an unsmiling face to the man.

"I am Lord Reath," he announced grandly. "I am sure that there was a mistake when my good friend Miss Whately requested the loan of a horse and was given this sorry excuse for an animal instead."

The ostler looked narrowly over at Sara. "Well now, my lord . . ." the man began with a sneer curling his lip.

"You will give her a mount fit for a lady, my man, and you will do so immediately." Lord Reath's tone of voice would brook no argument.

The ostler's gaze shifted quickly back to Lord Reath, and then without another word, he spat out some orders to a groom who was standing nearby. The young man led the nag back into the stables and returned a few minutes later with a much more respectable looking gray mare.

"That will do for today, but in the future, I expect this lady to be given your best horse each and every time she calls upon this establishment."

The groom had led the mare to the mounting block and Sara climbed up onto her back. Lord Reath mounted his horse once again and without another word followed Sara from the stables.

The mare whinnied in protest and Sara loosened her tight grip on the reins.

"I thank you, sir," Sara said through her gritted teeth, as they made their way back to the park.

"That is the most insincere thanks I believe I have ever received," Reath observed, mildly.

"You will excuse me for not being properly elated that you were able to do something that I was not, simply because you have a title. Or do you think it is because you are a man? Which was it that impressed the ostler more, your enormous size and presence or your exalted personage?"

"You will forgive me if I chose not to answer that question, Miss Whately, since I see no way of doing so without causing even more offense than I obviously have already," he answered quietly.

Sara felt a tinge of regret for her harsh words, but she had become so angry when he had been able to do what she had not. She began to think of her independent lifestyle in Philadelphia as some sort of fantastic dream. How was it that there she was able to run an entire household alone, and yet here in England she could not even walk down the street or rent a hack by herself?

Her morose thoughts were interrupted by the approach of a gentleman driving a high-perch phaeton with a beautiful high stepper pulling it.

"Ah, my Lord Reath, I see that you are once more taking advantage of your close association with this lovely young lady," Beau Brummell called as he drove up to them.

Sara pulled her mount to a standstill, as did Lord Reath.

"But this time, I must really insist upon an introduction," Brummell said, smiling, but with a very calculated look at Sara.

Lord Reath did not look particularly pleased, but had no choice but to comply.

"Miss Whately, may I have the honor of introducing Mr. Brummell?"

"How do you do, Mr. Brummell," Sara said as mildly as she could.

"Your servant, Miss Whately," Brummell said, standing for a moment in order to bow to her. "I do hope you enjoyed your little stroll down St. James the other day?" he asked with a twinkle in his eye.

"I am afraid that I had quite lost my way. Luckily, Lord Reath was there to redirect me," Sara tried desperately to hold her temper in check. She knew she was being baited, and did not wish to rise to it.

"Ah yes, how fortuitous that he was there. Had you and Lord Reath already been acquainted, Miss Whately?"

"Yes, as a matter of fact, we have met on a few other occasions."

"I say, Brummell, is it not a little early for you to be out and about? It was my understanding that you did not rouse yourself before noon," Lord Reath said, raising one of his slashing black eyebrows.

Mr. Brummell smiled, but it was not an entirely pleasant one. Shaking her head, the mare reminded Sara, once again, to loosen her grip on the reins.

"You are quite correct, my lord. Unfortunately, an affair of honor forced a departure from my usual habits today. And what of you, Reath? How is it that you are about so early? You are not in your evening clothes, so you couldn't possibly be on your way home from the evening's entertainments . . ." Mr. Brummell's voice trailed off suggestively.

Reath's cheeks turned slightly pink. "No, despite my previous reputation, I no longer engage in such behavior."

Sara wondered if he were deliberately

telling her this as well. Considering his conduct the previous evening — leaning so close to speak to that woman — she had suspected that he was quite a rake. But now he was telling her that he was one no longer. Was this, perhaps, what upset her aunt whenever Lord Reath's name was brought up, his past reputation? She supposed that it very well might be.

"Miss Whately, I hear you are staying in town with your cousin, Lady Darlington?" Mr. Brummell continued with his questioning.

"Yes. She is bringing me out this season."

"Ah. And what of your parents? You are from America, are you not? How is it that they let you travel all this way all alone?" Brummell asked.

Sara looked askance at Mr. Brummell. Enough was enough. Sara felt like a prisoner of war under questioning, but there was no reason why she should stand here just to satisfy this incredibly rude man's curiosity. She smiled sweetly.

"I am from America, Mr. Brummell, where people have the freedom to move about as they please, either alone or with others and entirely without fear of being questioned by . . ."

"Brummell, if you will excuse us, I believe it is time I escorted Miss Whately to her home," Lord Reath interrupted.

Sara turned her furious gaze on to Lord Reath. How dared he interrupt her? She was just about to lay into this overbearing, patronizing fop.

Lord Reath gave her a warning look and turned his horse back in the direction of the gate. Sara had no choice but to follow his lead. With barely a nod of farewell and her head held high, she followed him until they were out of earshot of Mr. Brummell.

"You seem to think, sir, that I have absolutely no ability to care for myself," Sara said, trying desperately to control her anger.

"I do beg your pardon, Miss Whately, but that is not the case at all. I merely . . ."

Sara pulled up her horse and turned toward the man.

"You merely interfered once again in my life! You think that I am some naive little girl who needs constant rescuing — but nothing could be further from the truth."

"I assure you . . ."

"No, sir, I assure *you* that if you continue to insist on attempting to save me from every unpleasant encounter that I become involved with I will . . . I will never speak to you again. And I will tell everyone I meet what a horrible, devious, interfering rogue you are!"

She spurred her horse and trotted off toward the gate.

He had done it again! He was trying to rescue her from making another blunder. He was trying to control her and her life. It was too much. She did *not* want his rescuing. She did *not* want his interference. She did *not* want him in her life!

If only there were some place where she could race her horse! She looked across the neatly manicured lawns where children were playing under the careful eye of their governesses. And then back at the path she was on, which was quickly filling up with pedestrians, horses, and carriages. She desperately needed some place to take out her pent-up emotions, but this was definitely not the right place.

What made it worse was that she was sure that Reath would know of some place where she could do just that, but there was no possible way she could go back to him now to ask. No, she would simply swallow her bile and continue home as quickly as she could.

Eleven

Her aunt's home was no better.

The front door was opened for her by Coddles, her aunt's butler. A more dour man Sara had never encountered. He frowned at her as she stomped through the door.

It took a great deal of self-control for Sara not to go running up the stairs. She took a deep breath and walked slowly, in a ladylike fashion, just as her aunt had insisted. She then opened and closed the door to her bedchamber without a sound, although she was sorely tempted to slam that door as hard as she could.

Annie peeked out from the armoire, where she had been hanging the first of Sara's new clothes, just arrived from the modiste. She stood staring at Sara for a good minute with her eyes narrowed before saying anything.

"There's something wrong. You're not behaving angry, but I can see by your eyes and the flush on your cheeks that you're fit to be tied."

"Annie, I have been neglecting my duties," Sara said, ignoring her maid's comments.

"In what way, Miss?"

"I have allowed myself to be diverted from my true purpose for being here in England by my aunt's desire to launch me into society."

"But, Miss Sara, you agreed that you would play what you called 'the society game' for a while before trying once again to go to Wyncort."

"Yes, and I have, haven't I? I went to that silly ball last night. I allowed my aunt and Lord Reath to introduce to me to all sorts of boring people with whom I attempted to have a rational conversation — against all odds, I might add. What more do I need to do before I can refocus my attention where it is needed most? When can I stop having to put up with meddlesome, interfering annoying people and do what I want — no, *need* — to do?"

Annie just stared at her with a rather sad look about her eyes.

"Annie, *you* must understand that I need to do this. If I do not, I don't know what will happen to my papa — to us all." She took Annie's hand in her own. "How long do you think he can continue writing articles for money? He is getting old, Annie, and no matter how much I would like to, I simply do not have the talent he has for stringing words together on a page. If I do not find my grandfather's jewels . . ."

"But, Miss Sara, you don't even know that they are truly there."

"My grandfather gave directions on how to find them. Of course they are there," Sara scoffed.

"Your father didn't think so. He said your grandfather was mad."

"Papa was simply upset at the time. I believe that the treasure is there and I am going to find it."

"Well, and what are you going to do with them once you've found the jewels?" Annie said, going back to her work.

Sara stopped and watched Annie fold the last of her new fine linen shifts and place the pile of them carefully into the drawer next to her new corsets and stockings. Sometimes her maid came up with the most insightful questions or observations.

"What am I going to do with the jewels once I've got them? Well . . ." Sara thought for a moment. "I've got to sell them, of course. But who am I going to sell them to? that is the question.

"Annie, could you do some discreet

questioning of the other servants? Find out where someone would sell some jewelry if they needed money. There must be a pawnbroker that someone knows."

"You want *me* to find out?" Annie's voice squeaked.

"Yes. If I were to ask, I would simply be told to apply to my aunt for money, or get questioned about why I wanted to sell off my jewelry. But you can ask without anyone thinking it odd. I am certain of it. Oh, Annie, you've got to do this for me." Sara took the maid's hands in her own and gave her her sweetest pleading look.

Annie had never been able to resist it. She nodded her head nervously. "All right, Miss Sara. But I don't like it."

"Good. Now I just need to find a way to get to Wyncort."

Sara began to pace back and forth, trying to think. But she kept bumping into pieces of furniture. Her bed, her bureau, the dressing table. She could not stand it. She suddenly felt claustrophobic.

She opened the door and went out into the hallway. A maid was passing by with a pile of clean linen. She stopped and gave Sara a brief curtsy before slipping past her in the narrow corridor.

Sara went down to the ground floor and

looked toward the front door. Coddles frowned at her. She turned and walked toward the back of the house, but nearly ran into a footman carrying a tray of tea things on his way up to her aunt who Sara supposed was in the drawing room.

After letting the footman pass, she went out into the small garden in the back of the house. It was a pretty garden, as town gardens went. There was a small flower bed and a tree with a bench wrapped around the trunk, but there was little room for anything else.

The high walls surrounding the garden seemed to close in on Sara as she stood there surveying the space. And then the gardener came in through the back gate, gave her a nod, and proceeded to weed the flower beds. She just could not be alone in this place! Sara paced the walls once and then went back inside, feeling no better.

Her mind repeated the same thing over and over again, coming up with no conclusion. How was she to get to Wyncort? How was she to get into Wyncort? How could she possibly leave London when she and her aunt had only just arrived?

Was there some excuse she could give Aunt Deanna that would allow her to return to Darlington? Could she say that she had forgotten something? That she was not feeling well and needed fresh country air? Would her aunt believe such a faradiddle when she knew that Sara had lived her whole life in a city? No. No. No. And certainly not.

Sara walked back through the house, avoiding another maid and Coddles's frowns. She stopped outside of the drawing room, caught by the sound of her aunt and Lord Alston's voices. They had not closed the door properly.

"Deanna, what will you do if you run into Reath again?"

"Oh dear, Justin, I do not know." Her aunt sounded quite agitated. "I cannot avoid him. He is as welcome as any in all the best drawing rooms."

"Yes, I believe the word has very quickly spread that he has reformed his ways, so that he is now even more sought after than before he left for India."

"So what am I to do?" Aunt Deanna asked again. "What do I say if he asks me once more about Sara's family? He has every right to ask, you know. Why, it is what any young man would want to know before wooing a girl properly."

"Naturally. The question is why he would want to woo Miss Whately. That is not to say that she isn't a very pleasant girl, and quite pretty, but you must admit that her manners are not . . ."

"Oh no, Justin, honestly. She just needs a little training, that is all. I am certain that she will catch on very quickly. Why, even Lord Reath said last night that society will merely think her an original."

"I am very pleased to hear that he thinks so, but I cannot help but think that Reath has something else in mind other than wooing Miss Whately. Not, I assure you," he added quickly, "that I believe his intentions toward your niece are not completely honorable. It is just that I cannot believe that it is Miss Whately herself that he is interested in."

This last statement confused Sara to such an extent that she wished she could ask Lord Alston to clarify himself. For what other reason would Lord Reath pursue her, if not to woo her? Not that she wanted him to woo her, she quickly told herself.

A more annoying man there never was. Why, he always had to take charge of whatever situation they were in. But then again, he did usually know what he was doing. And it had felt rather wonderful having someone care for her, rather than the other way around. But no — what was she thinking? He was an overbearing rake. She did not want the man's attentions.

Sara knew that she was perfectly capable of caring for herself. She did not need a man to take charge of her life. And besides, then she would not be able to find her grandfather's jewels and save her family's fortunes. She was sure that were Lord Reath to find out what she was up to, he would put an immediate stop to it — and then where would she be?

Three days later, she found herself leaving her aunt's home to pay a morning call at Lady Merrick's. The first morning dresses of her wardrobe had finally arrived, and her aunt, after having spent days teaching her proper behavior, had insisted that Sara join her.

Sara followed her aunt out to their awaiting carriage, and found that she was becoming rather nervous despite all of her lessons the previous week. Sara was sure that her aunt would not be able to poke her with her fan or signal her in any other way when she strayed on to some unacceptable topic as she had at Lady Bantam's ball. No, it would be entirely up to her to do and say the right thing — and so she would, she decided.

Lady Merrick's classically decorated drawing room was only slightly over-crowded, but not so much that it was uncomfortable. As Sara and her aunt were greeted by their hostess, she could not stop herself from looking around to see if Lord Reath was present.

She spotted him leaning against the mantelpiece beside Lord Merrick. After three days of not seeing Lord Reath, Sara was struck once again at how incredibly handsome he was. He quite stood out from the rest of the gentlemen present. Even his good friend, Lord Merrick, was not nearly as good-looking.

When he wasn't smiling, Lord Reath had a look of the stern, forbidding aristocrat, with his slashing eyebrows, straight mouth, and steel gray eyes. But then he would smile and laugh and his entire face would change. A dimple appeared in his cheek and his eyes crinkled just a little at the corners and exuded a warmth and cheer that sent Sara's heart fluttering.

"My dear Lady Darlington, it has been an age!" Lady Merrick said, drawing Sara's attention away from Lord Reath. "And this must be your cousin, of whom I have heard so much."

"Indeed, Lady Merrick, may I present Miss Sara Whately?"

Sara smiled and said all that was proper, as her aunt had taught her.

A small nod from Aunt Deanna, and Sara knew that she had done well.

"Lady Merrick, do you know of any dancing instructors for hire?" her aunt asked. "It was quite a shock to realize that dear Sara has not learned how to dance. I cannot for the world imagine what my bro . . . cousin has been about, to raise his daughter this way!"

"Indeed, I know of the most marvelous dancing instructor. Monsieur LeCarreau is most talented at teaching all the latest dances. He has been teaching my daughter, Georgette, for some time. She will be ready to make her come-out next year. Remind me, and I will get you his card before you leave."

"I knew you would be the one who would know — so very helpful!"

"I am happy to be of assistance." Lady Merrick turned away to greet another person who had just entered the room.

Sara and her aunt made their way to a group of ladies sitting around a tea tray. They were about to sit down when one elderly lady said very loudly, "So this is your young cousin who doesn't know St. James from Piccadilly, eh, Lady Darlington?"

The other ladies laughed, and Sara felt her face heat with embarrassment. Even after three days away from society, they still remembered her mistake as if it had happened the day before.

Her aunt forced out a laugh as well. "Indeed, the poor dear got all turned around."

"Hear the gentlemen got quite a good look at her as she stood outside of White's."

"I could not say." Lady Darlington's voice sounded very strained.

"Well, what have you got to say for yourself, gel?" the old lady taunted.

Sara raised her chin. "I say that the gentlemen who sit in that bow window are nothing but a group of supercilious meddlers to pass judgment on everyone who walks by. And the way they stare is extremely rude. I, personally, don't give a fig for anything that they say or do."

Sara immediately realized she had done it again. The shocked stares of the other ladies were enough to make her want to crawl under the rug and stay there.

Then she was struck with the most horrible thought — if Lord Reath had been at hand, he would have known precisely what to say. And he would have known to stop her before she could open her mouth, just as he had the other morning when she was speaking with Beau Brummell.

She stole a glance over at him as he stood deep in conversation with yet another gentleman on the other side of the room. He hadn't really meant to intrude in her life, only to be sure she didn't embarrass herself.

A wave of guilt washed over Sara for the horrible way she had treated Lord Reath when he had only meant to help her. He had been all that was kind and good — getting her a better horse and then making sure that she didn't get herself into trouble, as she had just now. And she had raked him down for interfering in her life. Perhaps she *needed* someone to interfere in her life, just a little — to help her in society, since she really did not know how to go on.

She supposed she owed him an apology. It was a disheartening thought. The idea that she needed help from others was humbling. She was confident, however, that she would soon learn to deport herself properly. She only needed to set her mind to it. The problem was that she really had no inclination to do so.

Sara noticed Miss Collingwood sitting at the far side of the circle. She was one who certainly needed no assistance in how to behave properly. Aunt Deanna had pointed her out to Sara at the ball the other night as a model young lady. She was also known as one of the reigning incomparables. With her beautiful blond hair, perfect complexion, and the most unusual golden brown eyes, Sara did not wonder at it at all.

So why was she sitting there with her hand covering her mouth, desperately trying to hold back a fit of laughter and not entirely succeeding? Sara moved over toward her, fully aware that every eye was still on her, and sat down next to the beautiful creature.

The young lady looked truly pleased that Sara had sat down next to her. She swallowed her giggles, set her mouth into a proper smile, and said, "You are Miss Whately, are you not? I am Julia Collingwood." She held out her hand and Sara was pleased to shake it.

The older ladies had by this time all put their heads together and were probably whispering furiously to each other about her impertinent speech. Sara deliberately ignored them.

"I appreciate that you are willing to speak with me after I thoroughly embarrassed myself. If ever I would wish to turn back the hands of time, it is now."

"Oh, no! You simply said what everyone else has been thinking for the longest time. I quite admire you for being so brave as to speak your mind."

"Really? You are not just saying that to be kind?"

"Oh no, truly," she said with so much honesty in her voice that Sara had no choice but to believe her.

"But I know that I should not say such things. I am surely going to get myself into quite a lot of trouble if I continue to do so," Sara said with a certainty she wished weren't true.

"Yes," Miss Collingwood said slowly. But then a large grin covered her face and her eyes twinkled with mischief. "Either that or you will become known as an original. Would that not be wonderful? Then you would have all the gentlemen swarming around you like flies to honey."

Sara couldn't help but laugh at the excitement in Miss Collingwood's face. "It would be wonderful . . . if I wanted to attract gentlemen."

Miss Collingwood looked completely

confused. "Do you not?"

"No. Honestly, I have no interest in marrying. I am only here because my father and my aunt insisted I have a season. Do you want to marry?"

"Of course I do. I thought every young lady wanted to marry."

"Oh, no. I was quite happy living with my father the way we were and truly wish my aunt had never convinced him to send me here." She paused, realizing once again that she had said too much.

"Please, Miss Collingwood, I should not have told you that," she said quietly. "Lady Darlington would be most upset if she found out that I have no intention of marrying — especially after all the money she just spent on buying me a new wardrobe and the time she has given me trying to teach me to behave properly."

"Oh no, I would not dream of telling anyone, honestly." She looked up from their conversation and nodded to a woman across the room. "You must excuse me, Miss Whately, that is my mama. I believe she is motioning for me."

Sara looked over at the slender woman who had been speaking with Lady Sefton. It was clear that she was Miss Collingwood's mother, for the similarity between the two was striking.

"It was very nice meeting you. I do hope that we will have an opportunity to meet again," Miss Collingwood said as they stood up and began slowly walking over to the two ladies.

"I hope so as well," Sara said earnestly.

Miss Collingwood stopped and turned back to Sara. "Will you be at home tomorrow?"

"I believe so. I'm unsure as to what my cousin's plans are."

Miss Collingwood took a quick look over her shoulder at her mother and then turned back and leaned close to Sara. "I will try to pay you a visit tomorrow and we will talk further then. I have never met anyone as brave as you," she said, her eyes twinkling once again. She then quickly turned around and schooled her expression into a polite, bland smile.

Sara stood stunned by Miss Collingwood's sudden confidence. She was going to pay her a visit? She thought her brave? Sara nearly laughed. If only she knew that it was stupidity, not bravery, that compelled her to act as she did.

"She is lovely, isn't she?" Merry said quietly, almost to himself.

Reath had his eyes on Miss Whately. She was trying to locate her cousin, after the young lady with whom she had been speaking had moved away. Without moving his gaze, he readily agreed with his friend's assessment.

"Her hair is such a pretty shade of blond. Almost red, and yet most definitely blond. And her eyes — have you ever seen such lovely golden brown eyes?"

Reath looked over at Merry, as he lounged against the side of the mantelpiece. "Who are you talking about?"

"Why, that young lady over there, talking with Lady Sefton." He nodded his head in the direction of Miss Whately's friend. She did indeed look to be a model of feminine beauty, in her white morning dress with a wide blue sash around the high waist. "Who did you think I was talking about?"

"Oh. I was looking at Miss Whately."

Merry looked over toward the center of the drawing room, where his mother now stood conversing with Lady Darlington and her young cousin.

"Ah, er, yes, she is pretty enough, I suppose. But much too petite for my taste. Now this young lady is definitely a good height for me, and a good everything else as well."

Reath laughed.

With a sigh, Merry turned from admiring the young lady. "How goes your wooing of Miss Whately?" he asked.

Reath stood away from the mantelpiece and raised an eyebrow at his friend. "I am *not* wooing Miss Whately."

"Oh no? Then what do you call it when you dance attendance on a young lady constantly for two days running?"

"I have not seen her at all for the past three days, and I call it assisting her as she is new to London and society. Besides which, it was your idea and Huntley's that I escort her and Lady Darlington the other night."

"Ah, right." Merry nodded his head wisely even as his lips twitched with mirth.

"You may stop that immediately. I can assure you that I have no intention of wooing her. I am not ready to get caught in the parson's mousetrap just yet, and even if I were, Miss Whately is not one I would consider to be a pleasant lifelong partner."

"Didn't insult you again, did she?"

"Yes, as a matter of fact she did. When I ran into her while riding in the park the other morning, I saved her from making a cake of herself in front of Beau Brummell."

"Not exactly grateful for your help?"

"No." Reath scowled in Miss Whately's direction. She was still conversing with Lady Merrick, but the expression on her face looked more like a grimace than a smile. She was clearly at pains to appear pleasant and amiable.

"You know, Merry, it is very rare that I've ever seen her really smile," Reath said thoughtfully after watching her for a few minutes. "And I don't believe I've ever heard her laugh or seen her truly happy. She is a very serious young lady." He pushed his hair back off his forehead, where it had fallen as usual. "She never seems to have any fun."

"What are you getting at? You are planning something, my friend. I can see it in your eyes."

Reath tried to look as innocent as he could. "I? Planning something?" Then he smiled. "Yes, perhaps I am."

The young lady Merry had been watching followed her mother to where Lady Merrick was standing. It looked as if she was about to leave. Miss Whately's smile immediately changed to a true smile as she and the blond girl exchanged a few words.

Merry quickly set down his cup of tea on the mantelpiece. "You will excuse me, Sin.

I must be introduced to my beauty before she disappears out of my life forever."

Reath laughed as his friend made straight for his mother and the young lady.

He moved to the tea tray that was set out near a group of older ladies and helped himself to a piece of buttery cake.

"I wonder if she is related to the Whatelys of Sussex. With behavior like that, I would not be surprised at all," Lady Farmingham was saying to Mrs. Saxton in a voice just loud enough to be heard only by those close to her.

Reath moved a step closer so that he could hear her friend's reply.

"She must be. Surely you remember the scandal with that other young Miss Whately?" Lady Farmington continued, not waiting for Mrs. Saxton to reply.

"When was that?" Mrs. Saxton asked, her rheumy eyes straying toward her friend.

"About . . . I suppose twenty years ago, it must have been, wouldn't you say, Clorisse?"

A bland-looking middle-aged lady nodded her head. "It was precisely twenty years ago, in 1791."

"Clorisse remembers everything. She is so useful to have about," Lady Farmington said.

Mrs. Saxton squinted her eyes in thought and then dabbed at them with her handkerchief. "You mean Elizabeth Whately, the one who ran off with, who was it, to America?"

"Yes, that's the one. She ran off with Wynsham's son." She sat back with a self-satisfied smile. "Never heard from them again, not even when Wynsham died."

"Surely with manners like that . . ." Mrs. Saxton clucked her tongue. ". . . this young one is certainly related."

Reath moved away, leaving the ladies to their gossip. Was it possible that Miss Sara Whately was related to Miss Elizabeth Whately, or Lady Wynsham, as he supposed she was now? It would explain why Miss Elizabeth Whately would have been willing to run off to America, if she already had cousins living there. And it would explain Miss Sara Whately's connection to Lady Darlington. They must be cousins by marriage.

This was all fascinating, but none of it helped Reath find out any more about the current Lord Wynsham's direction. He needed to speak with Lady Darlington again. She had not been very helpful when he had mentioned her brother at Lady Bantam's ball, and then they had been interrupted before he could get to the heart of the matter. He would definitely need another opportunity to speak with her.

Sara noticed Lord Reath had moved to stand once again by the fireplace, but Lord Merrick had abandoned him. She quickly moved to his side before he could strike up a conversation with anyone else.

"Lord Reath, might I have a word with you?" she asked nervously.

She was rewarded with a bright smile that she knew was completely unwarranted, considering her behavior toward him the last time they had met.

"Of course, Miss Whately. Would you care to take a turn about the room?"

Sara nodded and tucked her hand into the crook of his arm, which he held out to her. "You are exceedingly kind. I do not deserve such kindness, especially after what I said to you in the park."

"Do not even consider it," he said lightly, with a wave of his hand.

"But I do consider it, sir. I have considered it a great deal since then, and I have come to realize that what you did was much more than I deserved. You could have let me make a fool of myself once again, but you did not. I am deeply indebted to you."

A small smile played on Lord Reath's face — not quite enough to cause his dimple to appear in his cheek, but enough to warm Sara right down to her toes.

"I . . . I am afraid that I am not used to needing any assistance from anyone in any form," she said hesitantly. "But you have shown me nothing but kindness and . . ."

"Please, my dear Miss Whately, say no more. I entirely understand. It is difficult to be in a new situation where you are unsure of the rules. I encountered the same thing when I first arrived in India. I knew nothing of the Indian rules of behavior, and even the Englishmen I encountered there seemed to live by different rules than those we have here. I, too, managed to make a fool of myself on more than one occasion. But I quickly learned what was acceptable and what was not, and I am sure that you will as well. You are an intelligent woman."

Sara felt a lump form in her throat, but swallowed it firmly. "Thank you, sir. You are very kind."

She then quickly excused herself before she began to truly make a fool of herself.

Twelve

Sara concentrated on Monsieur LeCarreau's feet. He went over the steps again, showing her how to move gracefully through the complicated figures of the country dance.

She wanted to make sure that she got it exactly right. After the fiasco at Lady Bantam's ball, if she ever mustered up the nerve to attempt to dance in public again, she wanted her dancing to be absolutely perfect.

The sound of voices outside in the hall disturbed her. Her aunt came into the room followed by a number of people, with Lord Reath in the lead.

"My dear, look who has come to join you in your lessons!" she said a little nervously.

"Ah, gentlemen and more ladies! Zat is just what we need!" Monsieur LeCarreau said, clapping his hands together. "But zis is pairfect, Lady Darlington, pairfect!"

Lord Reath bowed to Sara, saying, "I do hope you will not mind the intrusion, Miss Whately. We all happened to meet and decided that we must pay you a visit. When your cousin kindly informed us that you were having your dancing lesson, we could not help but take advantage of her generosity and join you. You see, we are all sadly in need of some brushing up of our dance steps."

"Yes, indeed," Lord Merrick agreed, giving Sara his usual bright smile.

"Haven't had a dancing lesson for ages," Mr. Fotheringay-Phipps drawled.

Sara curtsied to the gentlemen and then was introduced to Lord and Lady Huntley. Lord Huntley gave her a warm smile as he bowed to her, and Lady Huntley was quite effusive in her greeting, giving Sara's cheek a kiss and her hand a squeeze. They were a very handsome couple, both strikingly beautiful. His dark skin, black hair, and bright turquoise eyes certainly stood out in the crowd, and she was certainly one of the prettiest women Sara had ever seen — with a perfect peaches-and-cream complexion, blond hair, and sparkling blue eyes.

"Ah, but now we 'ave too many gentlemen," Monsieur LeCarreau lamented. "Lady Darlington, you will 'ave to 'elp even our numbers."

"I will sit out," Lord Merrick offered.

"Oh yes, oh dear, that is very kind of you, my lord. I am terribly sorry," Lady

Darlington said, as she took her place opposite Mr. Fotheringay-Phipps in the line of ladies.

Monsieur LeCarreau then once again went over the steps, although this time rather more quickly than he had done with Sara. The pianist started to play — and immediately Mr. Fotheringay-Phipps began to turn the wrong way.

Lord Reath burst out laughing. "Fungy, old boy, I thought you of all of us would be better coordinated," he teased. The Huntleys and Mr. Fotheringay-Phipps himself began to laugh as well, and Sara could not help but join in.

"My apologies. I was too dazzled by the beauty of all the ladies around," Fungy said with a straight face. "Shall we begin again?"

They did, but this time Lord Reath was too busy watching to see if his friend would make another mistake. He was not properly paying attention to what he was supposed to be doing, and began to make mistakes as well.

"My apologies, Lady Darlington," Reath said with a rather unrepentant grin as they both turned the wrong way.

Meanwhile, Lord and Lady Huntley were adding to the chaos. Instead of standing still at the end of the line as they were supposed to, they were holding hands and flirting with each other. They were so involved with each other that when it was finally time for them to join in the dance, they completely missed their cue and the entire dance had to be begun all over again.

"Huntley, we know you are newly married, but really!" Lord Merrick said with mock severity.

Lord Reath burst out laughing again, and Lady Huntley, although turning a very becoming shade of pink, also could not hold back her giggles.

As they began again, the mistakes and silliness began anew as well. And soon the whole mood was more of that of a romp than a dancing lesson. The sound of roars of laughter and feminine giggles almost drowned the tinkling of the pianoforte.

Sara found herself laughing until her sides ached and she had to stop and catch her breath. She had not had so much fun since . . . well, she could not think of when she had ever had so much fun.

Lord Reath's voice cut into her thoughts. "Miss Whately, if you would take my left hand, no my right, I believe we shall turn as we ought."

"Oh, yes, I am sorry, I was woolgathering."

Sara looked up at him while taking his hand and felt the oddest sensation. All of a sudden, despite all the cheerful crowd around them, it was as if there was no one else in the room but herself and Lord Reath.

His deep gray eyes twinkled merrily at her, but there was something else there, something exciting and disturbing both at the same time. Heat rushed up her arm from her fingertips and coursed through her body as she felt her bare hand being held gently, but firmly in Lord Reath's own hand.

She knew that at a proper dance they would both be wearing gloves. Now she knew why. What she was feeling as she and Lord Reath held each other's hands was positively indecent.

And his eyes. She could drown in those eyes . . . so deep, so enticing. They looked like the sea on a stormy day.

"Miss Collingwood!" Cuddles's deep voice was heard distinctly from the doorway, despite the laughter and music in the room.

Sara started. Her face flooded with heat and she pulled her hand away as if she and Lord Reath had been doing something improper.

She rushed to her new friend's side so that she could both greet her and get away from Lord Reath. His proximity did something to her and she desperately needed to regain her composure. Her head began to clear immediately.

"Miss Collingwood, how lovely that you could come. Won't you join us?" Sara said, leading her friend further into the room. Her aunt seconded her invitation.

Miss Collingwood's eyes took in everyone present, including the dancing instructor and the pianist. A broad smile lit her face as her eyes shone with excitement. "A dancing party? What fun!"

"Well, it was supposed to be my lesson, but it has rather turned into a party," Sara said looking around.

"Yes, indeed, a rather impromptu one I am afraid," Aunt Deanna said.

"Otherwise, I would certainly have invited you yesterday," Sara added.

The introductions were dispensed with quickly and Lord Merrick could not have looked more pleased to partner Miss Collingwood. From the slight flush on Miss Collingwood's face, she too was very well pleased with this situation.

Monsieur LeCarreau quickly described the way the dance worked now that they had four couples, and then the music began again. But Miss Collingwood's arrival did nothing to change the mood that had prevailed, as the silliness began again, initiated by Lord and Lady Huntley, who forgot that they were no longer the last couple and did not join in the dance when they should have. Laughter rang out and soon even Miss Collingwood, who was clearly an excellent dancer, was making silly mistakes.

Sara was deeply disappointed when the hour was over and Monsieur LeCarreau called an end to the lesson. She walked with Lord Reath to the door as she saw everyone out.

Miss Collingwood left walking with her maid, and the others piled into a cabriolet. Before joining his friends, Lord Reath turned to Sara and took her hand. Sara felt her knees turn to water as he pressed his lips to the back of her hand without removing his eyes from her own. Once again his eyes had turned stormy gray.

He did not say a word, but his look conveyed all his meaning. He had truly enjoyed himself and looked forward to seeing her again, soon. Sara's heart filled with joy, but she did not know what to say either.

And then he was gone. As soon as he

had leaped into the carriage, it started off.

Sara floated on air all the rest of the day. She could not say what she did or what the cook had served for dinner. All she knew was that she had had the most wonderful afternoon of her life.

It was not until she climbed into bed that night that her conscience began to bother her once more. Time was so precious to her, and she had lost all sense of it while drowning in those stormy gray eyes.

Reath strolled lazily around Lady Stokes's drawing room. The musical portion of the evening had finally ended with a grand finale of all the Stokes sisters playing together — Miss Stokes on her harp, Miss Caroline on the pianoforte, Miss Constance on her violin, and the youngest, Miss Cressida, with her cello. If only they had had a modicum of talent it would have been bearable, but, sadly, not one of them did.

Reath joined Merry at the refreshment table. "You owe me for this," he growled softly.

"Yes, I know," Merry smiled and tried hard not to laugh. "But isn't Miss Collingwood looking absolutely stunning tonight?"

Reath sighed and looked over at the

young lady sitting with her mama. This evening she had on a pale peach-colored gown that complemented her light brown eyes and brought out the pink in her cheeks. She did look very beautiful, as even Reath had to acknowledge.

"This afternoon's dancing was perfect," Merry said, not removing his gaze from Miss Collingwood.

"Yes, it was precisely what I had been hoping for. I am sure I could not have planned it better had I tried." Reath reached for a lobster patty. "I would like to do something else tomorrow. Something completely different."

Merry finally turned away and looked at his friend. "Still trying to woo, er, entertain Miss Whately?"

Reath frowned at him for a moment, but then his expression lightened. "Yes, of course. Perhaps a trip to the British Museum? What do you say?"

Merry's eyes went wide. "You want *me* to go to the British Museum? You cannot be serious, Sin."

"We shall invite Miss Collingwood along, of course." Reath nodded in the girl's direction.

Merry looked back at the young lady and then nodded slowly. "If you can get Lady

Ardmouth to agree, I will go. But remember, if Miss Collingwood doesn't go, neither will I. That is simply too much to ask."

Reath smiled. "Not a problem."

He picked up a glass of ratafia and one of lemonade and walked over to where Lady Ardmouth and her daughter were sitting.

"Lady Ardmouth," he bowed to her and then handed her the wine. "Miss Collingwood, you are looking lovely this evening," he said, handing her the lemonade.

The two ladies took their proffered drinks and nodded to him. "Good evening, Lord Reath," they said, nearly in unison.

"Lady Ardmouth, I am planning an informative outing to the British Museum and I was wondering if I may be so bold as to request Miss Collingwood's company?"

Lady Ardmouth's eyebrows crept up her forehead. "You want to escort my daughter to the museum, my lord?"

"Yes. But not alone, I assure you. It will be an unexceptional outing in the company of Lord Merrick and perhaps Lord and Lady Huntley as well."

"Lord Merrick is to go?" Miss Collingwood asked quickly.

"Yes, of course," Reath answered, smiling at her obvious enthusiasm for his friend.

"Oh, Mama, may I please? I have never been to the British Museum before."

Lady Ardmouth considered the possibility.

"I assure you, ma'am, it will be entirely proper, and Lord Merrick and I will see to Miss Collingwood's safety and comfort the entire time." Reath winked at the young lady. "There is apparently a fascinating exhibit of Greek vases that is quite a sight to behold, and there are some Egyptian artifacts as well, I believe."

"Vases?" Lady Ardmouth looked at him skeptically.

"Yes, ma'am, vases. As I say, completely unexceptional."

"When do you propose to go?"

"Tomorrow afternoon at four — if that is convenient for you?"

The lady looked over at her daughter, who pleaded with her silently. She sighed. "Very well, you may go."

"Oh, thank you, Mama."

"Thank you, my lady. We will pick you up tomorrow then, a little before four." He bowed and then left them to return to Merry's side, triumphant.

Thirteen

The following day, at precisely four-fifteen, Reath's carriage pulled up to Lady Darlington's town house. He had written to Miss Whately's cousin that morning, asking her permission for Miss Whately to join them on their outing to the museum. Miss Whately herself had replied in a very pretty hand that she had been given permission.

He picked up Merry and Miss Collingwood first. Unfortunately, Huntley and his wife had been unable to join them. But still he hoped that the day would be a success, even without Lady Huntley's vitality or Huntley's thoughtful charm.

Miss Whately's face was flushed with excitement as he handed her into the carriage. "I am so exceedingly grateful that you have arranged this expedition, Lord Reath. I have been wanting to go the British Museum, but did not know when I would get a chance,"she said after he climbed in after her.

"Oh, Miss Whately, you cannot mean it?" Miss Collingwood asked, laughing at her friend.

Miss Whately looked confused. "But of course I mean it. Are you not looking forward to it, Miss Collingwood?"

"No, I cannot say that I am. I am afraid I find very little interest in looking at dusty old relics."

"But then why are you coming along?"

"Why, for the company of course." Miss Collingwood looked slyly up at Merry, who was sitting directly across from her.

"Oh." Miss Whately seemed to be a little uncomfortable at Miss Collingwood's boldness. She stole a look at Reath, and he could not help but wonder if she would have done the same as her friend had she been uninterested in the expedition.

He decided that it would be safer not to pursue that line of thought, and instead focused his attention on being as charming and entertaining as he knew how.

"I have heard that the most amazing things are exhibited at the museum. There are treasures from Greece and Egypt, the Rosetta stone — and I've even heard that they have an Egyptian mummy." Reath said, building on Miss Whately's attempt to entice some enthusiasm from their companions.

Merry laughed. "No, do they? That sounds positively gruesome. I assure you,

Miss Collingwood, that unless you very much want to see it, we will avoid that particular display."

Miss Collingwood smiled at Merry. "Thank you, my lord. I think I would very much prefer *not* to see it."

"Will you be brave enough to view it, Miss Whately?" Merry asked.

Miss Whately's eyes twinkled with mischief. "I am greatly looking forward to it, sir."

Reath found himself oddly pleased with her answer. She had proven her bravery to him before, but he was still thrilled with the prospect of a female who did not act in the least bit missish.

He hopped eagerly from the carriage as soon as they arrived, and then turned to help the ladies out. Tucking Miss Whately's hand into the crook of his arm, he proceeded into the building with a great deal more enthusiasm than Merry and Miss Collingwood, who trailed behind them.

"I am sorry, Miss Whately, but until recently they had guides who could tell you everything you wanted to know about each exhibit. I am afraid now you will simply have to make do with my shoddy memory from my school days," Reath said with a teasing grin as they entered the main entrance hall.

Sara's lips twitched, but then she deliberately sighed heavily and said, "Oh, that is a shame. Perhaps between the two of us we will be able to figure out what things are. I have read quite extensively, you know."

"No, I did not know. But I am very happy to hear it. Perhaps instead of my enlightening you, you may teach me a thing or two." Reath kept the tone of his voice light, but in the back of his mind he was truly impressed.

Miss Whately laughed. "Indeed, sir, I am certain that I will."

Reath answered her smile with one of his own. "Then let us proceed, Miss Whately. I am eager to learn."

Miss Collingwood and Merry followed them into the first room, but soon found a bench to sit on.

"Please go on without us, Miss Whately. I believe I am still feeling a bit fatigued from all that dancing yesterday," Miss Collingwood said, making herself comfortable.

"Are you sure? Should I stay and keep you company?" Miss Whatley asked her friend with real concern in her voice.

"Oh, no. I will impose upon Lord

Merrick to do that. If you will not mind too much, my lord?"

"No, no, not in the least." Merry could not have looked happier.

"I am certain that Merry will take proper care of Miss Collingwood," Reath assured Miss Whately as they continued on alone.

She gave Reath an understanding smile. "I am certain that he will."

Once again she took his arm and they continued on with their tour.

Reath managed to keep Miss Whately entertained as they strolled slowly through the museum, though there were times when he had to truly scour his memory for some tidbit of information or story about each exhibit. And he was even more impressed when she could add bits of information from her own store of knowledge.

They both found the Rosetta stone fascinating, and Miss Whately did not complain when he hurried her through some of the classical Greek sculptures that depicted the naked human form — both male and female.

But she did, in the end, agree with Lord Merrick about the mummy — it was gruesome. Reath thought so as well, but enjoyed the sensation of her hand holding tightly on his arm as they viewed the exhibit. He knew that she needed him to be strong for her and was more than happy to be placed in the role of protector.

They slowly wound their way back to the room where they had left Miss Collingwood and Merry.

"Have you been sitting here this entire time?" Miss Whatley asked as they approached them.

"Oh no, we got up and strolled around a little," Miss Collingwood answered.

"Are you feeling in need of a little refreshment, ladies? Shall we drive over to Gunter's for ices?" Reath asked.

"Oh, I would like that above all else," Miss Collingwood answered immediately, her eyes lighting up with enthusiasm.

"Miss Whately?"

"That would be wonderful," she answered with as much eagerness as her friend.

Miss Whatley sat back in her chair at Gunter's with a look of pure pleasure on her face after she had put her first taste of lemon ice into her mouth. "I declare, there is nothing more refreshing or delicious a treat than this," she said, filling her spoon with more of her ice.

"I am so glad that you are enjoying it, Miss Whately." Reath smiled at her.

If only he could make her this happy every day, he thought to himself. He then stopped himself. Never in his life had he wanted to be in one lady's company every day. Variety had always been his watchword.

In his youth he had had a different woman for every day of the week, and each week he would mix them up so as to not always visit the same lady on the same day. How could he even think about always only being with Miss Whately?

And yet, that is just what he had been thinking — how nice it would be to be with her — just her — every day. He could not even imagine ever getting tired of her, or bored. She was so fresh and unusual. Intelligent, with a quick mind and quick tongue.

And at this moment, she had the most beautiful smile on her face and laughter in her eyes. He always wished to see her thus.

Once again, Sara had difficulty sleeping that night. Lord Reath's smiling eyes haunted her as she tried to fall asleep. His laughter rang in her ears like some evil menace.

How could she have had so much fun? Why had she not been trying to find a way back to Wyncort? How could she have forgotten all about her father — her dear, dear papa who was all alone at home in Philadelphia?

She picked up his picture, which sat, as always, on her bedside table. What was he doing? How was he faring? Was he remembering to eat? Did he sell his last piece to the almanac so that there was money for food? And if he did, had he immediately invited all of his friends who were always hanging about to dine with him, so there was no food for the following day? How many times had Sara thought that she had shopped for three days only to find the larder bare again after only one?

Her beloved Papa. Generous to a fault. Sara smiled down at the picture, and brushed away the tear that threatened to drop down onto it.

But she knew in her heart that what was bothering her most was that she was truly having fun. In the company of Lord Reath, she felt light of heart and mind, carefree and liberated from any thought of responsibility and duties. Guilt assailed her.

Lord Reath made her feel . . . it was beyond wonderful, beyond happy, it was . . .

Sara couldn't place the feeling, but it was also not one that she had ever felt before. And, she told herself sternly, it was not a sensation that she liked having. How could she like feeling so giddily out of control?

If there was one thing that Sara had always been, it was in control — of her household and of her emotions. She took a deep breath, punched down her pillow, and determined that she was not going to allow anything or anyone to take her independence and her self-control away.

Sara sighed. Life would be so much simpler if only Lord Reath were ugly or unkind or uninteresting.

Fourteen

By the time the following evening had arrived, Sara's face, knees, and mind were all aching.

Sara and Lady Darlington had worked almost the entire afternoon in preparation for that evening, when Sara would attend a *ton* party. All of the high sticklers were expected to be at Lady Southworthy's soiree that evening. If Sara wanted vouchers to Almack's, she would need to be on her best behavior.

They had practiced Sara's smile — not too big or bold, but not too small either; her curtsies — the exact depth for each different degree of rank; and her conversation — what topics were appropriate to speak of and which were not. And they practiced them all again and again until Sara was tired and sore.

Towards the end of the lesson, Sara supposed, just to liven things up a little, her aunt also tried to detail for her the different types of gentlemen to be found in society — the Corinthian or sporting gentlemen, the dandy and the rake.

"Mr. Fotheringay-Phipps is a prime example of a dandy, and from what I have heard, Lord Merrick is quite the Corinthian," her aunt explained.

"And which type is Lord Reath?" Sara couldn't help but ask. She immediately reprimanded herself. She should not care which he was. She should not be interested in Lord Reath at all. Hadn't she decided last night that she would put him out of her mind?

But the damage was done, the question was out, and her aunt was trying to come up with an answer. "Well, in his youth he was quite the rake. No young lady of a good upbringing would go near him for fear of tarnishing her reputation. But he does seem to have reformed. And, oddly enough, he has proven himself a good friend to you."

"Why is that odd?" Sara asked. She was reminded of Lord Alston's assessment that Lord Reath was up to something. Could she get her aunt to open up about what worried her about Lord Reath? There was something important that she was not being told — she was sure of it.

Her aunt began to wave her fan in front of her heated face. "Oh, I am afraid cannot say, my dear. It is old history and perhaps it is best forgotten. You will simply have to use your best judgment when it comes to dealing with Lord Reath."

Sara wished her aunt could have been more helpful. Because, truth be told, Sara was not sure that she was able to follow her best judgment. Despite the fact that she had firmly decided last night to avoid even thinking about Lord Reath, she still had not been able to get him out of her mind and had ended up staying awake most of the night.

Descending from the coach that evening outside Lady Southworthy's house, her mind was still swirling — with thoughts of Lord Reath and anger at herself for not being able to follow her own resolutions.

As she, her aunt, and Lord Alston squeezed into the overcrowded rooms, she quickly decided that she would not encounter any difficulties with her manners. There was hardly room to stand, let alone carry on a conversation.

Lady Darlington took Sara's arm, and they proceeded to promenade around the room very slowly, her aunt nodding and smiling to acquaintances along the way. Every so often, they would stop and her aunt would introduce Sara to this lady or that gentleman. Sara, for the life of her, could not remember so many names, and she stopped trying after a short time.

A few names caught her attention — Jersey, Cowper, and Princess Esterhazy. They, she knew, were some of the patronesses of Almack's, and, according to her aunt, to be bowed and scraped to at every opportunity. Sara was annoyed with herself, as her nerves warred with her better judgment that screamed out that she was not there to appease these silly women. Still, she was careful not to say more than was necessary when she was introduced to these ladies — if only for her aunt's sake, not her own.

It seemed like they had been there for hours when they happened upon Lord Merrick and Lord Huntley, who were laughing together over some nonsense.

Honestly, Sara thought to herself, *those gentlemen are never serious.* Remembering all of the conflicting feelings she had fought all night long, Sara had a hard time presenting a pleasant demeanor. And here these men were smiling and laughing, without a care in the world. It was enough to make a girl scream.

"How do you do, Lady Darlington? And Miss Whately, what an honor it is to see you this evening." Lord Merrick bowed.

Sara focused her mind on pulling her mouth up into a smile. "It is a pleasure to see you both. I do hope you are enjoying this crowd — I mean, soiree?" Sara said.

The gentlemen laughed at her deliberate slip.

"Yes, indeed. Lady Southworthy must be thrilled to have such a crush," Lord Huntley said.

"I still don't understand how she manages to do so, year after year. It's not as if she provides even an adequate supper," Lady Darlington sniffed.

"And yet her soirees are all the rage. I even saw Brummell here a short time ago," Lord Merrick said.

Sara looked about, desperate to avoid an encounter with that gentleman.

"I must say, Lady Darlington, I have not had so much fun dancing as I did the other day," Lord Huntley said.

"Oh, indeed, my lord, it was quite wonderful how you all arrived at just the right time," Lady Darlington replied.

"Reath planned it just right. And we were extremely lucky to have Miss Collingwood join us as well," Lord Merrick said.

"Lord Reath planned it? How could he have done so?" Sara asked, clasping her hands together in front of her.

"Well, I do not know that he specifically planned for the dancing, but he certainly intended for there to be some amusement for you when we all called," Lord Merrick explained.

"Did he?" Sara felt her anger moving from a simmer to a slow boil. He had done this to her on purpose? "And how, precisely, did he unilaterally decide that I needed to be amused?"

"Why, we all need to have some fun sometimes, Miss Whately," Lord Reath said, joining their group. "You seemed to have an exceptionally good time at the museum yesterday as well," he reminded her unnecessarily.

Sara looked up at him towering over her. He was forced to stand very close to her, due to the crowd, and his proximity threatened to overwhelm Sara's senses. How was it that she did not feel this way the previous day? She had clutched on to him so tightly when they had viewed the Egyptian mummy, but then he had only felt good, making her feel cared for and protected.

Sara now looked at him standing so close she could smell his spicy and enticing scent of what Sara now knew to be sandalwood. She could not help but think how

192

easy it would be for her to simply rest her head against his broad chest and to be held safe within his strong arms. In his arms she could forget all about her troubles and her worries. The rest of the world would just melt away.

Her anger boiled over at her own seditious thoughts.

When she spoke her voice was low and menacing. "Perhaps, sirah, you feel the need for such ridiculous diversions, but I assure you I do not. You will kindly leave me out of your asinine amusements and allow me to decide when and how I shall find my own entertainment."

With that, Sara turned and strode away, her head held high.

Once again that damned man had interfered with her and her plans! Why could he not just leave her alone? No, instead he had to insinuate himself into her life and make her crave his embrace and his protection!

All he had to do was stand next to her, and all her years of independence disappeared as if in a puff of smoke. All her goals and dreams of making a better life for herself and her father flew out of the window . . . and all she wanted was to laugh, to have fun, and to be taken care of by his lordship.

She was so angry she could feel the blood pounding through her veins.

Miss Collingwood was standing nearby with her mama, talking with Lord Holyoke. Boldly, Sara strode up to them, eager to appear to Lord Reath to be completely at her ease and unperturbed.

"Good evening, Lady Ardmouth, Miss Collingwood," Sara said. She gave the lady a smaller curtsy than was warranted, owing to the fact that her knees were still shaking from her encounter with Lord Reath.

"Good evening, Miss Whately," Lady Ardmouth said, none too happy with the interruption.

Miss Collingwood greeted Sara with much more enthusiasm. "Miss Whately, how wonderful it is to see you. Do you know Lord Holyoke?"

"Yes, thank you, we met earlier this evening. I hope you are still enjoying yourself, sir? But, how could you not, when you are conversing with Miss Collingwood?" Sara said, giving her friend a warm smile.

"Indeed, Miss Whately, indeed. Delightful company," his lordship replied.

Sara's aunt joined them just then. To Lady Ardmouth, she gave a pleasant smile and greeting, but when she turned her eyes toward Sara, her smile stiffened, and she looked rather sad and disappointed.

"I do hope that you will forgive me Lady Ardmouth, Lord Holyoke, but I am afraid it is time my cousin and I took our leave. Come, Sara."

Sara had no choice but to follow her aunt. That lady managed to continue to smile and be pleasant as they slowly made their way out of Lady Southworthy's home and into their carriage. It was there that Sara got the earful she had been expecting.

"How could you, Sara! I have never been so mortified in all my life. To insult Lord Reath in that horrid way when all he was doing was trying to help you and entertain you. And right to his face! My word, have you no shame? Have you no conscience? Have you no idea of how you should treat your betters? He is a viscount, for heaven's sake! How could you insult him in that way? And in public, too! In front of his own friends. What happened to using your better judgment?" Lady Darlington took a deep breath and continued on in the same vein for the entire journey home.

Sara said nothing. For what could she say? Her aunt was absolutely correct. She should not have insulted the gentleman — but she had been so angry. Her words had slipped from her mouth before she could even think of anything beyond Reath's overwhelming presence.

Reath settled back against the soft cushion of the sofa in Merry's library, where they had all retreated at the end of the evening. After leaving Lady Southworthy's soiree, the four friends had had a look-in at the Putnams' musicale. But it had been deadly dull, so they had unanimously decided to forgo any more pleasures that evening and simply relax in Merry's spacious, well-appointed home.

Merry had done an excellent job in redecorating the room since Reath had last been there. It was now extremely comfortable, with an overstuffed sofa and a couple of wing chairs set conveniently in front of the fireplace. It was perfect for relaxation with a good book, or for sitting at one's ease with friends.

Reath put his stockinged feet up on the table in front of him. "Now I remember why I hate society — you have stand on your feet the entire evening," he said to no one in particular.

Fungy copied his pose from the other end of the sofa, and Merry sat sprawled in a chair facing them. Huntley was the only one still standing, as he was helping himself to a glass of brandy from the decanter on the table in the corner.

"What we suffer for a bit of entertainment," Fungy sighed.

"I do not see the entertainment in crowding into a few small rooms and suffering through a glass of horrible lemonade and a lobster cake. We only meet and greet the same people night after night. To what end?" Reath said.

"Sin, you've been away too long. There is no end. No point. It is just what we do," Fungy explained slowly as if to a child.

Huntley joined them, sitting on the matching chair to Merry's, and stretching his legs out. "I always thought it was for the ladies that we suffered so," he said quietly.

"It is, Julian. We go to enjoy the company of pleasant, companionable ladies, and not suffer the insults of thoughtless young chits," Merry said, looking at Reath.

"Rather odd, that. Thought she liked you," Fungy said.

"From her behavior the other day, we thought we would be hearing wedding bells in June," Huntley agreed.

"Oh, I don't believe she is thoughtless, Merry. It is just that her tongue seems to have a life of its own, and doesn't always check to make sure that what it is about to say is appropriate," Reath said, unable to stop himself from defending Miss Whately, even after what she had said to him that evening.

"There is a novel way to explain it," Fungy said.

"You are entirely too charitable, Reath," Huntley said.

"Yes, perhaps." He took a sip of his own brandy. "Well, I must say, I have never been given a set down by a woman before. I am not entirely sure how to react."

Reath ran his hand through his hair. "I suppose I must assume that yesterday's behavior was an aberration. Although she has shown moments of warmth, she has rarely been much more than cool in her behavior towards me. Rather indifferent, I believe."

"I never thought I'd see a female who was indifferent to you, Sin," Merry said.

"Indeed, neither had I." Reath thought about it for a moment, and then could not stop the smile from spreading across his face. "Do you know, I find it quite charming?"

"What?" Merry and Huntley said in unison.

"Can't be serious." Fungy said, sitting up.

"Odd, I know. But the idea of a young woman who has absolutely no interest in me at all . . . somehow I cannot help but find attractive."

He looked at the stunned faces of his friends. "Oh, come, she is attractive in other ways as well — she is incredibly beautiful, intelligent, and charmingly innocent. But I must say that I find her disinterest fascinating."

Reath grinned as he took in the openmouthed silence of his normally loquacious friends. "Lady Darlington asked me to call in the morning so that Miss Whately could have an opportunity to apologize to me properly. I gave her a rather noncommittal reply, but now that I think on it, I do believe I will go."

"You cannot be serious, Reath!" Huntley protested.

"Honestly, Sin, after that stinging set down, you are going to go back for more?" Merry said, laughing.

Reath let out a chuckle, appreciating the humor in the situation. "Oh, yes. I certainly should not go expecting anything resembling an apology, should I? Well, I will be the model of patience and goodwill. Perhaps I'll even invite her out for a drive in the afternoon. It is supposed to rain, I believe."

His friends all burst out laughing.

"Nothing more agreeable than getting

caught in the rain with an offensive young lady." Reath paused, thinking out his plan. "Nothing more romantic either," he added quietly.

Without a word, Annie began to help Sara undress for the evening. She worked silently, and Sara could not decide whether to confide in her maid or not. Annie had always been a voice of reason and had guided Sara through some of her more difficult times, but would she understand about the confused feelings she had for Lord Reath?

Sara sighed. There was only one way to find out.

"I am almost convinced that Lord Reath has somehow become aware of my plans," she began.

Annie stopped unbuttoning the back of Sara's dress. "Why do you say that, Miss Sara?"

"I learned this evening that our little impromptu dance the other afternoon was entirely of Lord Reath's making. He came here with all of his friends, determined to create some sort of diversion for me."

Sara stepped out of her dress and turned her back to Annie so she could untie her corset. "And then again yesterday, Miss Collingwood and Lord Merrick had absolutely no interest in the museum. They sat and talked the entire time without looking at a single thing. Lord Reath, on the other hand, kept me distracted, looking at all of the artifacts on exhibit.

"Now why do you think he would do that if he did not know that I had other plans? Why would he be so interested in entertaining me if he did not know that I needed to leave London and return to Wyncort?"

"I could not say for certain," Annie said resuming her work. "Perhaps he just wanted you to have fun."

"Yes, but why? It is incomprehensible, Annie. Either he knows that I have another goal in mind other than marrying, or there is something in particular that he is after. Lord Alston thinks that Reath is up to something, and now I am certain of it as well."

Silence reigned for a few minutes while Annie slipped Sara's night rail over her head.

"Tell me what you have learned about selling the jewels," Sara said, resuming their conversation as Annie began to brush out her hair for the night.

"There is a man," Annie began hesitantly.

"Yes? You have learned of someone who will buy them?"

"There is a man who has a house on Drury Lane, just behind the theatre. He is known to buy unwanted jewels for a fair price."

"Oh, excellent! We will go there to-morrow morning."

"Oh no, Miss Sara. Surely not. It is not at all proper for you to see him. Apparently, it is not a safe neighborhood. I was warned not to go there alone, if I had to go at all," Annie said, pulling at Sara's hair as she braided it.

"Annie, calm yourself. You will not go alone. We will go together. Surely between the two of us, we will be safe enough. And I must go to see that he truly exists and is willing to buy what I will have to sell." Sara gave her maid's arm a reassuring squeeze. "Fret not, Annie. It will be fine. We will go early in the morning and we will never be missed."

Sleep was once again long in coming. Only this time, it was Lord Reath's shocked and hurt expression when she had insulted him that stayed in front of her mind's eye. Oh, why couldn't that man just leave her alone!

Fifteen

Doing as she was bid the following morning, Annie approached James, the footman who stood at the door, and sent him off on a fictitious errand for her mistress. As soon as he had left his post, Sara came quickly down the stairs and the two of them slipped out the front door.

Looking around to make sure she was not spied by anyone she knew, Sara walked down the street at a quick pace, with Annie trotting along behind her. At Piccadilly, she hailed a hackney, and the two hopped in before anyone could recognize them.

As the cab pulled up to the address Annie had supplied, Sara began to feel her first stirrings of trepidation. This was indeed an unsavory neighborhood.

She made sure her veil was completely covering her face before she stepped down from the carriage. Ignoring the boys who immediately moved closer to see what a lady of quality was doing in their neighborhood, she rapped at the door and hoped that it would be answered quickly.

It was, immediately — and she was sorry

for it. An enormous man, even larger than Lord Reath, filled the doorway. He was as tall as the door and nearly as wide. It was not fat that made him wide, but by the looks of it, pure muscle. Sara held her reticule tightly to stop her hands from shaking.

"May I 'elp you?" he asked in a deep, rough voice.

"Yes, I am here to see Mr. Green," Sara said, trying not to let her voice show her fear.

" 'Ave you an appointment?"

"No. I was not aware that I needed one."

The man frowned at her and seemed to try and think for a moment. Finally, he came to a decision as Sara looked around nervously behind her.

"You better come in. I'll see if 'e can see you. Your name please, Miss?"

"Oh, er, I would rather not give my name, if you do not mind."

This did not seem to surprise the giant at all, and he nodded and moved to the back of the house.

Sara stood in the entry hall and looked around. The house was clean, if nothing else. A bare wood floor ran down the narrow hall toward the back of the house, and a stair ran up the wall to the right.

Within a very few minutes, the giant came back. "Foller me please, Miss."

Sara nodded and followed the man back into the darkening recesses of the house. She could feel Annie sticking close behind her, clearly too nervous to let her mistress leave her side.

Stepping through the indicated door, she was pleasantly surprised by the handsome office in which she found herself. It was not very large, but the light streamed in through the window. A man sat at a desk in front of the window, using a magnifying glass to inspect some stones on a black velvet tray.

She stood for a moment, waiting for his attention. When he was satisfied with the stones, he turned and stood up to greet her.

Sara was surprised at the man's height, which could not have been above four feet. When he had been sitting behind his desk, it had seemed as if he were much taller.

He looked her over shrewdly, gauging, perhaps, the quality of what she had to sell by the quality of her clothes.

"Although it is not very frequent, I have received calls from ladies of quality, but usually much older ladies. What is it that brings you to my humble abode?"

Sara cleared her throat. "I hope to be in possession soon of a number of fine pieces of jewelry from India," Sara began nervously. "I would like to sell them as quickly as I can for as much money as I can. I was told that you were the person to see."

The man nodded his head slowly. "What sort of jewelry? Loose stones, necklaces, bracelets, earrings? What sort of stones? Diamonds, emeralds, rubies?"

Sara swallowed. "I . . . I do not know yet. I have not seen them myself. I have only heard that they are there. I . . . I must retrieve them and then I can bring them to you."

"Where? How are you going to retrieve them? Are they yours?"

His questions came fast and Sara began to become a little annoyed. It was none of his business where they came from, only that they came and that he bought them.

She lifted her chin. "That is none of your business. You only need to know that they are mine and I want to sell them. You, I presume, will buy them?"

"I can make no promises. If they are indeed yours to sell, I will make my decision to buy them or not when I see them. It depends on what there is and what sort of market there is for your trinkets."

"These will not be trinkets, I assure you. It is my understanding that there is a treasure in jewels, and I will accept only a substantial amount for the lot of them."

"You will accept whatever I offer. You have no other choice." His voice was suddenly loud and commanding.

Sara clutched at her reticule again and took a deep breath. "I do have a choice. I need not sell them to you at all. If you do not give me what I feel to be a fair price, I will not do business with you. Good day, sir." Sara turned to go.

The man slipped between her and the door. A wily smile on his face made chills go up Sara's spine. "Bring your jewels to me when you get them and I will see what they are worth. I will give you the best price I can, I assure you."

Sara nodded and then quickly walked around him and out the door. The hackney she had hired was still waiting for her outside the door as she had requested, and she was never so relieved to get back into the smelly carriage.

Reath quickly turned his back and walked down the street. He did not want Miss Whately to know that he had followed her. Luckily, she was so involved in making sure that she herself was undetected that she did not look around. Instead, she kept her head down so that her veil and the brim of her hat covered her face well.

As the hackney pulled away, Reath crossed the street and knocked at the door of the same house. A hulking man answered and Reath slipped inside before the giant could say anything.

"I would like to see the gentleman with whom the young lady just met," Reath said.

Perhaps it was the steely look in his eye, or the edge in his voice, but the giant unquestioningly led the way back to an office.

The man seated behind the desk looked rather surprised, possibly unaccustomed to having such frequent visitors of quality. He was silent for a moment, taking his time to look Reath over. But Reath was not going to stand for such insolence. Without hesitation, he strode up to the desk and leaned on it, putting his face close to that of the man.

"What is your business with Miss Whately?"

The man sat back in his chair and steepled his hands together. "I believe that is between myself and the young lady. Unless you are her husband?"

"I am not, but you will tell me what she was doing here. Now." Reath began to move around the desk in a deliberately threatening way.

"You know that within a moment I can call my man from the front, and you will be out the door without further ado," the man said coldly.

"You will tell me your business with the young lady," Reath persisted, ignoring his threat.

The man looked at Reath towering over him, and wisely decided to tell the truth. "She came to inquire about selling some jewels."

"Jewels? Where did she get these jewels?"

"She did not tell me. Only that she was soon going to be in possession of a treasure in jewels from India. She said that she does not have them yet, but that she would be getting them soon. She would not say from where."

Reath moved back, allowing the man some relief from his menacing presence. He needed to digest this information.

He had just come back from India, but he had not brought any jewels back with him, aside from a few trinkets he had purchased for his mother. Where did Miss Whately expect to get this Indian treasure?

He returned his attention to man behind the desk. "Listen to me, and listen well. You will not buy anything from that young lady. If she offers to do business with you, you will refuse. Is that clear?"

"I am afraid I cannot do that."

"You can, and you will — or you will suffer for it. That young lady is not to be admitted to this house again. Understood?"

"But . . ."

"If she comes to call with her jewels, you are to turn her away and then contact me. I will see that it is worth your while." He tossed one of his visiting cards on the desk and then strode from the room.

Merry was still at breakfast when Reath called. Fungy was there as well, but this did not surprise Reath. He was not entirely sure that Fungy did not live at Merry's house half the time. The two cousins were very close.

With very little preamble, he related the events of the morning.

"Where do you think Miss Whately is going to get a treasure?" Merry asked as soon as Reath had finished his tale.

"I cannot imagine. I also do not understand why she would need so much money," Reath answered. He bounced a spoon against the table. He had been much more upset by this discovery than he was willing to let his friends know.

When he had seen Miss Whately steal away from her home in a furtive fashion, he had been curious. But when he had followed her into a dangerous neighborhood, he had begun to get angry. To have exposed herself to such dangers as lurked there with only the protection of her maid was foolhardy.

Concern was now warring with his anger. There must be a very good reason for her to have risked both her life and her reputation to seek this man out.

"Has a decent dowry from Lady Darlington," Fungy said, as perplexed as the others.

"Perhaps she doesn't want Lady Darlington's money? Wants to pay her own way? But that doesn't make sense." Merry stroked his chin.

Reath shook his head. "I just don't know, but whatever it is, it cannot be good. Perhaps she is in debt at home, in Philadelphia?"

"Got to find out, Sin," Fungy said with conviction.

"Yes, but how? When? We would need to be alone in order for me to question her — and even then I could not possibly ask her outright."

"No, but you were always good at finding out information without anyone suspecting what you were doing," Merry said. "I have full confidence that you will learn what you need to know."

Sixteen

"I know I should not encourage Lord Reath's attentions, but I cannot let such a slight go unheeded," Lady Darlington said.

"No. I too cannot like his persistent attentions, but . . ." Lord Alston shook his head sadly. "I just do not know what you are going to do about that girl."

"If I had known how my brother was raising her, Justin, I would have insisted that he send her to me earlier," Lady Darlington said, clasping her hands together.

"You are too good, Deanna," he said, gently taking her hands in his and massaging the worry out of them.

Sara cleared her throat to make her presence known. She had slipped into the room unheard as soon as she had sent Annie off with her cloak and hat.

Lord Alston immediately dropped her aunt's hands and stood up from the sofa the two had been sharing.

"Sara! Where have you been, my dear?" Aunt Deanna asked, sounding worried.

"I am sorry, Aunt, I went out for a walk. I felt the need for some exercise," Sara lied. "I had Annie with me."

"Well, thank goodness you have learned that much. Still, Sara, you should not simply leave the house without telling anyone. We were all quite worried when we discovered you missing."

"Aunt Deanna, I am sorry to be such a bother to you. I do not mean to be, honestly. I will try to do better."

Suddenly, inspiration hit Sara and she put on her most apologetic expression. "Perhaps if I could have a week or so at Darlington to practice more and learn the social graces better, I would not embarrass you so?"

Lady Darlington looked at Lord Alston to see his opinion of this idea. It seemed for a moment as if she were finally inclined to accede to Sara's suggestion, but Lord Alston did not agree.

He looked at Sara with his mouth turned down. "No, I do not believe that would serve the purpose. What you need, young lady, is a chance to mend your ways. And, although it is very tempting to send you into the country for a few weeks as punishment, I do not believe it would serve the purpose."

He walked over to the fireplace, contemplated the fire for a moment and then turned around. Crossing his arms in front of his chest, he assumed a very commanding stance.

"It is better that you confront Lord Reath and apologize to him at your earliest opportunity. He is clearly so disgusted with you that he did not even show up this morning as your aunt had asked him to. But that does not mean that you will not have another opportunity to behave as you should."

Sara's hands interlocked tightly in front of her. "He was asked to come over this morning and he did not?"

"No. But as I say, we will provide you with one more opportunity to apologize, and you will do so." Lord Alston's voice was firm.

Sara wondered if Lord Reath had come over and had witnessed her slipping away. But she had looked around to make sure she was not spied. Could she have not seen him? No. It was not possible to miss seeing someone so large as Lord Reath. Lord Alston must be correct in his assumption that Lord Reath simply did not come.

Lady Darlington interrupted Sara's musings. "I know! I will host a Venetian breakfast!" she exclaimed.

Lord Alston turned to her with a smile.

"An excellent idea, my dear."

"Yes, a Venetian breakfast at the Botanical Gardens. There Sara will have an opportunity to apologize. We will invite all of his friends, Miss Collingwood and her mama, Lady Ardmouth. And perhaps some other young people as well."

Lord Alston nodded. "It is decided."

Sara was exceedingly relieved when Miss Collingwood and her mother entered her aunt's drawing room that afternoon. Until then, she had had to politely suffer through the same humiliation and embarrassment again and again, as the *ton*'s gossips delighted in rehashing both Sara's walk down St. James, as well as her ride in the park on a broken-down nag.

She escaped to greet Miss Collingwood and pulled her off to the window seat, where the two of them could sit and talk privately.

"I cannot tell you how happy I am that you are here, Miss Collingwood. Not only am I pleased to see you, but now I no longer have to listen to those horrible gossips rehashing all of my foibles and faux pas."

"Oh dear, you poor thing. Well, I shall certainly not do anything of the sort. But you must call me Julia, and if you do not mind, I shall call you Sara."

Sara gave her friend a warm smile. "Thank you, it is so much nicer that way. Now, do tell me how you enjoyed Lady Southworthy's soiree last night. Am I correct in my assumption that you were happy for my interruption while you were talking to Lord Holyoke?"

Julia laughed. She had a very pretty, very genteel laugh, more like the trill of little bells. "How well you read me, Sara! Indeed, I was. I am afraid that I find Lord Holyoke entirely too much the dandy for my taste."

"I completely sympathize with you."

"There were, however, a few gentlemen present whose company I enjoyed. And one whose company I would like to be in much more frequently, if only the rules of Society would allow it," Julia said with a twinkle in her eye.

"Yes? And who might that be?" Sara asked with feigned innocence.

"Well, I enjoyed speaking with Lord Branough, and Mr. Wrightsley. They are both very pleasant gentlemen. Of course, Mr. Fotheringay-Phipps is always amusing. I also had a chance to speak with Lord Reath." Julia paused and gave Sara a searching look before continuing. "But I was especially pleased to have a chance to speak with Lord Merrick."

Sara tried her best to give her friend a knowing smile. "You are very fond of Lord Merrick, are you not?"

"I have to admit that I am. He is all that is wonderful. So handsome and kind and yet funny and lighthearted. He lives up to his nickname, Merry."

"Yes, he truly is quite merry. You two seemed to have had a very enjoyable time at the museum, even though you did not stir once from your bench."

Julia had the grace to flush. "And you, Sara? Did you meet any gentlemen last night who interested you?" Julia asked, but then added quickly, "I know you have no interest in marriage, but still you must have enjoyed the company of some gentlemen?"

"Oh, yes, I found one or two gentlemen who were quite pleasant to speak with," Sara said.

"Did you have a chance to speak to Lord Reath, perhaps?" her friend asked innocently.

Sara felt her face get a little warm and knew she was beginning to blush, but it was not for the reason Julia thought. "I . . .

I am afraid that I did not have a very pleasant conversation with Lord Reath."

Julia looked concerned. "Oh, I am sorry. Can you tell me what happened — or would you rather not?"

Sara looked down at her hands clenched in her lap. "I found out that he had orchestrated the impromptu dance party we had here the other day, because he felt that I needed some amusement."

"Did he really?" Julia looked very happy.

"Yes. But, I am afraid, I have a very quick temper, and it flared and I gave him a rather stinging set down."

Julia was silent for a moment. "But why? He was doing something nice for you by arranging some amusement. Why would you give him a set down for that?"

Sara did not raise her eyes from her hands, but quickly blinked back the tears that momentarily blinded her.

"I do not know. Perhaps because I am not used to people doing things like that for me. I felt that he was trying to interfere with my life. But, indeed, I now see that you are right, Julia. He was only trying to be nice. He has been exceedingly kind to me, and I have done little else than be rude and insult him." She gave her friend an apologetic smile.

Julia grabbed Sara's hands and held them tightly in her own. Sara was so grateful for her strength and friendship that she nearly began to cry in earnest.

"If you will excuse me, Julia," Sara whispered, not entirely trusting her voice, "I believe I need a moment to compose myself."

She gave her friend's hands a squeeze and then rushed from the room. Up in her own bedroom, she stood at the window looking blindly out at garden behind her aunt's home.

He was not trying to control my life, he was only being kind. And she had rewarded his kindness with a rude insult. How many times now had she done this horrible thing? How many times would he keep coming back, keep helping her out of awkward situations, keep trying to make her smile and be happy?

She looked up at the sky, trying desperately to stop the rush of tears that threatened to burst through.

He cared about her, he defended her and made her happy. He made her feel protected and . . . a horrible thought suddenly occurred to her.

I love him. How could she not when he was so kind and wonderful?

Her heart felt like it was overflowing with emotion. She turned back to face her room, and then her eye caught sight of the small portrait of her father sitting on her bedside table.

Moving over to it, she picked it up and caressed the loving face of her papa. He was all alone at home, without her to care for him. Despite all of her plans, she had done nothing, nothing at all toward easing his financial straits.

Placing the picture back on the table, she squared her shoulders. Her tears flowed from her eyes, but Sara knew that she could not afford to allow anyone, not even Lord Reath, to interfere with her goal.

She could not afford to fall in love. It was out of the question.

There were more people than Lord Reath and herself involved here — there was her father and Annie, both of whom depended upon her for their welfare. She could not, would not, let them down.

Sara poured some cold water into the basin on her washstand and splashed it onto her face. She would put Lord Reath and her love for him from her mind and concentrate on finding a way to Wyncort.

It was her only hope.

Seventeen

Sara somehow managed to avoid seeing Lord Reath for much of the following week. But there was no way to avoid him at her aunt's Venetian breakfast.

That morning, Sara had woken up to bright sunshine and cursed. It was a perfect day for a picnic. She had been hoping that the rain from the past few days would continue, making it impossible to hold their planned excursion. But it was not to be.

An animated party gathered at the park early that afternoon. Reath and his friends were in fine form and had many of the guests nearly in stitches at their hilarious recollections of various Venetian breakfasts of the past.

"In all, Lady Darlington, I think your breakfast today is top of the trees," Reath concluded, while making a grand leg toward their hostess.

Lady Darlington laughed appreciatively. "Thank you, my lord. You are exceedingly gracious, and I am happy if my small efforts today have given you some diversion."

She looked around at all of her guests and said, "Now do not feel restrained to stay just within this small area. Please feel free to go for a walk through these lovely gardens. Enjoy the day."

There was a general assent and many young ladies, along with their agreeable male escorts did just that.

Reath noticed that Miss Whately was standing next to her aunt, watching various couples go off to walk the paths of the garden.

"I would be honored, Miss Whately, if you would consent to join me in a stroll about," he said, giving her a little bow.

She looked to her aunt for permission. The lady smiled and nodded her head and then said in a rather serious voice, "Remember, Sara."

Miss Whately bit her lower lip and nodded before taking Reath's outstretched arm.

Seeing many of his friends taking the path immediately to their left, he chose instead to take the path to the right.

They walked in silence for a few minutes.

"I would like . . ."

"These are . . ."

They both started at once.

"Oh, I am sorry, sir, you were saying?" Sara said quickly.

"Nothing of any import. What were you going to say, Miss Whately?"

She looked away for a moment and then turned back with a determined look in her eye. "I wanted to apologize for what I said the other night at Lady Southworthy's soiree. I should not have been so rude. I realized later, as usually happens with me, that you had meant well and that I had reacted without thinking it through. I am very sorry."

Reath could not hide his smile. She looked so utterly repentant and beautiful that he did not have the heart to reproach her. Even if he had been made upset by her harsh words, he could not have said so at that moment.

"I entirely understand, Miss Whately."

"Do you, really? I felt sure that you would. You have seen my temper in action before, so I was hopeful that you would understand that it was simply a fit of pique which made me say such dreadful things."

"Yes, that is just what I thought."

"I did truly enjoy dancing with you — and our trip to the museum was quite wonderful," she said quietly.

"I enjoyed spending the time with you as

well. How is it that you managed to escape childhood without learning to dance?" he said, deliberately turning the subject.

She shrugged and looked a little worried. "I never had the time — and, to tell you the truth, I don't believe my father ever thought of giving me dancing lessons."

"What of your mother? Did she not dance either?"

She found the ground fascinating once more. "My mother died when I was very young."

A stab of hurt for the girl bit into Reath's chest. "I am sorry."

Bravely, she forced her smile on to her lips. "It is quite all right. I was only six when she died, and don't really remember her very well."

"I suppose it was very difficult for your father, for he not only had to cope with her loss, but had a daughter to raise as well."

"You might think so, but my father never took any pains to raise me. In fact, quite the opposite." She gave a little laugh. "It was I who felt the need to look after him after my mother died, not the other way around."

"But — you were six! Surely you had a governess or some other lady to look after you?" Reath asked.

"No. I had no one. Except Annie, that is — my maid. That is why I never learned any of the social graces, I am afraid."

"What a free and easy childhood you must have had, then. I was always burdened with governesses and tutors throughout my youth," Reath said, trying to keep a hint of jealousy from his voice as he thought of the restrictive atmosphere in which he had grown up.

"Were you? I never thought of it as free and easy. Quite the contrary." She was silent for a moment as they walked on slowly.

She then took a deep breath and said quietly, "My father has never had very much money. The reason he never hired a governess for me was because he could not afford to do so. We only ever had Annie to help with the cooking and cleaning."

Reath wanted to commiserate, but bit his tongue to stay quiet. She must be getting very close to the reason for selling these jewels she claimed to have.

"And yet, he has always felt it beneath his station to actually work for a living. He prefers to write for his own pleasure rather than to earn money. So it has always been up to me to make sure that whatever we had would last until . . . until he next got the inclination to write something that he could sell to a newspaper or a journal."

"Beneath him? I do not understand, how could that be so? Did he come from a wealthy family? I am afraid I do not know much about the Whately family's circumstances."

"Oh, my father is not a Whately. Actually, that was my mother's maiden name. When my father moved to America, he wanted nothing more to do with his family, so he took his wife's name rather than her taking his."

Reath was shocked. He had never heard of such a thing. "Your father's family must have done something truly horrible to elicit such a response!"

"It was not really his family, but rather his father. He refused to allow my parents to marry, which led to them eloping to America in the first place. His mother used to send him money so that we could live without my father having to work."

Her voice dropped to little more than a whisper, so that Reath had to strain to hear her. "But then, about ten years ago, my grandfather lost our family's only estate in a game of cards. That was the end of the money. Both my grandparents died very soon afterward, and since then my father has been forced to sell his writing to earn money."

Reath quickly put the facts together in his mind. Her mother's name was Whately, and her grandfather had lost his estate in a game of cards! It all made sense in a horrible, gut-wrenching way. Reath nearly laughed at the irony.

"Your mother — her name wasn't possibly Elizabeth, was it?"

Miss Whately looked up at him in surprise. "Why, yes, it was."

Reath stopped walking. "That would make your father Lord Wynsham."

Miss Whately stopped and looked up at him, frowning. "Yes, it would, if he had not repudiated his title."

Then her face cleared, and she laughed. "Oh, I am sure that you are shocked that my grandfather was a titled gentleman since I have so often insulted you for being one yourself. But, honestly, that is where I learned my prejudice. My father has had nothing good to say about the aristocracy. He is quite a staunch republican, you know, and he still insists on using my mother's maiden name as his own."

Reath swallowed hard. "Yes, I see. It is completely understandable that you feel the way you do."

He still could not get over the agonizing story of her childhood. Losing her mother at such a young age, living in poverty, and managing the household finances as a child, making things last until her father could earn more money. Reath's own childhood had not been a happy one, but at least he had never had to worry about where his next meal was going to come from.

It was no wonder that Sara was a serious young woman.

And her unhappy life was entirely his fault.

If he had only returned the estate immediately, or not accepted it at all in the first place, her family would never have had to live in straitened circumstances. Why had it taken him ten long years to return what had never been rightfully his in the first place? He did not need the income from the estate.

But Sara had needed it, desperately.

He had to make this up to her, somehow. He had to do something to give her back the childhood she had lost because of him. And with it, a full life as an adult as well.

She had the capacity to laugh and have fun — had she not proven so? But she was clearly still worried about her father having enough money with which to live. If he could only remove all of her worries, shoulder her responsibilities . . .

Of course he could! He could do precisely that if she married him. He certainly had enough wealth so that she and her father could live comfortably for the rest of their lives.

He stole a glance over at Sara. She still looked sad and worried. He ached to smooth away the frown from her beautiful forehead.

He wondered what she would say were he to ask her to marry him right now.

No. It would be best to bide his time a little more. She clearly felt a warmth toward him, but he was not certain that she liked him enough to marry him.

And, at the same time, he could not but help but think of his parents, and of their loveless marriage. He had promised himself at a young age that he would only marry for love. But that was long ago, before he had ruined someone's life. No, the only thing to do, the right thing to do, was to marry his dear, sweet Miss Whately — Sara.

He just needed to woo her a bit more, and then he would ask her to marry him, and then he would never see that worried look on her lovely face again.

Reath ran his hand through his hair and began to plan.

The silence between them dragged on. Sara looked up at Reath and watched the conflicting emotions cross over his face. She had said too much. She could not believe how much she had revealed to him. It was her love for him that had made her do it, she knew. She had to stop this. She had to stop it immediately.

Well, perhaps she had solved her own problem. He clearly had a thorough disgust of her now. She could see it in his eyes, which were usually so warm and laughing. Now they were cold and serious. His beautiful smile was nowhere to be seen either. His face was closed and forbidding.

He had seemed so sympathetic and trustworthy. He had cared for her, and she wanted nothing more than to be looked after by him. It had never seemed a burden to look after her father and their household until she had met Reath and experienced for the first time what it was like to be cared for and looked after by someone else. But now, he would do so no more, she was sure of this.

"Miss Whately, would you and your aunt

care to join me on a little jaunt I am planning?"

"I am sorry? A jaunt?" Sara was thrown off guard by his sudden interruption into her thoughts.

"Yes. I thought perhaps I would put together a little party and go into the countryside one day next week. Nothing very elaborate, but there is a little inn I know of that has the best food you could possibly imagine and some lovely ruins nearby that we could visit."

"That sounds very nice, sir. I am sure that my aunt and I would be honored to make up one of your party."

"Excellent. I shall make the arrangements."

Sara looked at Reath. His eyes were not on her, but on the horizon, and his brow was furrowed. Despite his pleasant invitation, she felt that he had suddenly moved far away from her in his mind.

Perhaps it was for the best. She was no weak, silly female who had to rely on men to care for her. She was strong and independent. She did not need him.

Sara straightened her spine and held her chin up.

She would just continue to be pleasant to him, for her aunt's sake. And if he did come to hate her for her poverty, perhaps he would leave her alone, and she could get on with her duties toward her father. She would find a way to Wyncort and get those jewels so that her father would never have to work again.

She did not need Lord Reath and she did not want him — or so she told herself.

Eighteen

"I do hope it will not rain, my lord," Lady Darlington called out from the open cabriolet where she sat with Miss Collingwood.

"You echo my sentiments exactly, my lady," Reath called back.

"Past few days have been dreadful with it," Fungy said, pulling his horse closer to the carriage. "Lucky we've gotten a dry day."

"Well, I am certainly grateful for this respite from the rain," Miss Collingwood said, clearly enjoying the outing. "I was so pleased when I received your note this morning, my lord, saying that we were going ahead with our plans despite the lack of sun today. I do so hate being cooped up inside the house for so many days on end."

Sara smiled over at her friend from the mare she was riding, and Reath felt his lips curve at the evident warmth between the two. "It has only been three days, Julia."

"I know, but I dare swear it feels like it has been a week!"

"How do you like Lovely Lady, Miss Whately?" Reath asked, letting his mount fall back a bit so that he rode next to her.

"Oh very much, sir. Especially now that we have left the city," Sara said. She stole a glance at him and then turned back to looking straight ahead. "It was exceedingly kind of you to lend her to me for this outing."

"Not at all. I simply could not bear to see you struggling with one of those horrible hacks that stable has lent you."

Sara gave him a small smile. "I would not have taken one. I am sure it could not have made the journey."

Reath laughed. "No, I believe you are right. You seem to be a very competent rider."

"Thank you, sir. It is the one thing my father made sure I learned well as I was growing up, despite the fact that we lived in the city and owned no horses."

"It is an extremely useful skill to have."

"Yes, that is what he said. The hacks we were able to borrow in Philadelphia were docile, but at least they were kept in good condition."

She leaned down and patted her horse's neck. "It always makes me so angry to see horses kept like the one I borrowed the other day. It is the sign of an uncaring ostler."

"Indeed. It is a shame to see animals treated so. That one you had should have been sent out to pasture years ago."

"Yes."

Sara rode up once again so that she was beside the cabriolet. Reath did not understand why she was acting so reserved today, but he was determined that she enjoy herself. If she was uncomfortable with him, he didn't see how his plan to propose to her was going to work.

Flirting with women was never something he had had problems with until he met Miss Whately. He still could not understand her. Even after the closeness they had shared at her aunt's breakfast, how could she be so cold toward him?

He fell back a little more, so that he was riding beside Lord and Lady Huntley. He had noticed on numerous occasions that his new friend seemed to have an easy way with the ladies — and, considering that he was happily married, Reath thought Huntley would be the perfect candidate to set Sara at her ease.

"Lady Huntley, will you forgive me if I were to ask a favor of your husband?"

"Why no, not at all, my lord."

He bowed slightly toward her. "Thank you."

Huntley looked at him with an expectant smile on his brown face.

"Miss Whately does not seem to be entirely at her ease this morning. I was wondering, Huntley, if you might try drawing her out. I have attempted it myself, but I have a suspicion that whatever is making her uncomfortable has something to do with me."

Huntley raised his eyebrows. "I would be happy to do whatever I can to set her at her ease, certainly. Shall I perhaps try to find out what is wrong as well?"

"No," Reath said, perhaps a little too quickly. "No, just entertain her a bit. I do so wish to see her smile."

He paused, and then felt that his friend deserved more of an explanation. "I do not want anything to mar her enjoyment of the day," he added. "Whatever it is that is bothering her I want pushed straight to the back of her mind."

Huntley nodded and then moved up to ride beside Sara. Within minutes, he had her laughing at some witticism.

Reath breathed a sigh of relief.

"It will be all right, my lord. Julian will have her forgetting about whatever is bothering her, and then we can all be jolly."

He gave Lady Huntley a grateful look.

"Thank you, my lady, you are exceedingly generous."

Lady Huntley was absolutely correct. Between Huntley and his other friends, Sara was much more at ease by the time they reached the inn where they were to dine. She was even able to give him a smile and a gentle thanks when he helped her down from her mare.

He removed his hands quickly from around her slender waist, since he was sorely tempted to let them rest there longer than was strictly proper. Sara clearly felt the same as he did, for she turned away quickly, with her cheeks turning the most delightful pink.

The private parlor he had requested was perfectly situated overlooking the beautiful gardens in the back of the inn. Everyone was able to take their ease, and it was a merry group that enjoyed the roast duck, fresh venison, and a ragout of lobster, not to mention the numerous removes provided by the chef. Rissole and a lovely pudding with preserved pineapples and oranges finished the excellent meal.

"I believe there are some lovely ruins to be seen quite nearby," Reath said generally to everyone.

"I would enjoy seeing them," Huntley

said quickly. "Would you care to join us, my dear?" he asked his wife.

"Yes, indeed. I do love ruins, as you very well know." She shared a secret smile with her husband.

"I am afraid, after that wonderful meal, I would like nothing more than a pleasant little stroll about the town," Lady Darlington said.

"I would be more than happy to join you, my lady," said Miss Collingwood.

"It would be my pleasure to escort you, if you would not mind," Merry said quickly, giving Miss Collingwood a smile.

The young lady smiled shyly back at him.

"And I, as well," Lord Alston offered.

"The rest of us shall ride out, then?" Reath said.

Everyone seemed to be well pleased with the arrangements. There would be chaperons enough for both parties with Lady Darlington and Lord Alston staying with Merry and Miss Collingwood, and the Huntleys and Fungy riding out with himself and Sara.

At the same time, Reath was confident that he would have no problems separating himself and Sara from the others while they examined the ruins. She seemed to have forgotten about whatever it was that was bothering her earlier.

Despite the cloudy sky, the weather was quite pleasant and it felt good to get some exercise after such a heavy meal. The cart track they took provided for a pleasant ride. Meandering past some pretty cottages and a farm, they crested a hill where they all reined in their horses. Spread out before them were large open fields of green grass dotted with sheep — and beyond, rising up on a small hill, lay the remains of an abbey, for which they were bound.

It was a beautiful sight, and Sara sat quietly looking about her and taking it all in.

"I do not get many opportunities to go into the countryside at home. It is so open and green here," she said, taking a deep breath of the fresh country air.

"It is indeed a lovely country," Huntley agreed. "We have nothing like these open fields of grass back in India."

"No. I must say I did miss this when I was there. I saw only jungle or desert, with the occasional farm thrown in," Reath agreed. "But, no, nothing like this."

A broad smile blossomed on Sara's face and a twinkle appeared in her eye. "How about a race to the abbey?"

"I'm game!" Lady Huntley said, sharing

Sara's enthusiasm.

"Very well," Huntley said.

"Excellent sport," Fungy concurred.

"Ready!" Reath called out sharply.

"Steady!" He paused for effect.

"Go!"

They all took off at top speed, galloping across the field.

Reath knew he was in the lead right off — he had the fastest horse. But Huntley was not too far behind, and Fungy was ready to overtake him on his right. Out of the corner of his eye, he caught a glimpse of Sara coming up close on his other flank. He turned quickly to make sure that Lady Huntley was not being left too far behind.

Sara's exhilarated laughter caught his attention as she rode past him into the lead. He would let her enjoy her brief victory and then catch up to win. Fungy seemed to have fallen behind.

A stone wall separated the field where they were from a boggy-looking patch before the final ascent to the abbey. It was not too high a wall, and Sara was heading toward it at full speed, clearly intending to jump it.

Reath called out a warning. He did not trust the ground after the rain they had had over the past few days.

"You aren't chickenhearted, Lord Reath?" Sara called back.

"No, Sara, do not attempt it!" he called out desperately, but she laughed gaily and did not slow down.

He pulled his horse up and watched helplessly as Sara took the jump. The mare landed on the other side and then, just as Reath had feared, slid in the mud and lost her footing. The horse went down and Sara was thrown from her back. Within moments, the mare was back up on her feet, but there was no sign of Sara.

Reath spurred his horse forward, leaping from its back as he neared the wall.

"Sara!"

He leaped over the wall and found her lying unconscious.

Nineteen

Kneeling down, Reath brushed her hair away and cradled Sara's sweet innocent face in his hands. His heart pounded in his chest.

Was she dead? No, she could not be. He laid a hand on her chest very gently and felt the rise and fall of her breathing. He then felt along her limbs to make sure that nothing was broken.

He heard Huntley, Fungy, and Lady Huntley scrambling over the wall.

"Is she all right?" Lady Huntley said, coming nearer.

"Took that wall at top speed," Fungy commented.

"There is nothing broken that I can tell," Reath said.

Sara opened her eyes and peered up him. "My . . . my horse slipped," she whispered.

"Yes. I tried to warn you, but you must not have heard me," he said gently.

She tried to nod, but at the slightest movement she winced with pain.

"Where does it hurt?"

"Everywhere, but especially my head."

"I hope you do not mind, I have taken

the liberty of feeling your limbs and there doesn't appear to be anything broken. If you will allow me, I will carry you back to the inn where Lady Darlington can attend you."

"Thank you."

Reath ever lifted her as gently as he could. She was much lighter than he had anticipated, merely a pleasant weight in his arms.

He carefully climbed back over the wall, with a steadying hand from Huntley, while Fungy led her horse around to a break in the wall nearby. Huntley handed her up to him. Reath settled her in front of him, sitting across his lap, and gently rested her head on his chest. With him holding her in place with one hand and managing the reins with the other, together they all slowly walked back toward the inn.

She felt so good snuggled against him. If he hadn't been so concerned for her well-being, he was sure he would have been extremely uncomfortable having her in such an intimate position.

Reath inhaled deeply, letting her scent settle happily within him. Surely, she was not seriously injured.

But what if she is? a nervous little voice cried from the back of his mind. He would never be able to carry out his plan to marry her and make her happy. And it was vitally important that he do that.

I love her.

Where did that come from? Reath looked around. Huntley had ridden off to warn the others of Sara's mishap and to secure a room where she could lie down. Fungy and Lady Huntley rode by his side, every so often stealing concerned glances in his direction. Reath kept his eyes focused in front of him and flexed his arm, which had begun to get tingles in it.

Sara shifted, burrowing her head further against his chest. She sighed in an almost contented fashion. Reath could not kept the smile from his face.

If only they could stay like this forever.

He did not know when it had happened, but at some point in this peculiar relationship, he had fallen in love. And he dared not even speculate on what had made him do so. It could not be that he actually liked being spoken to so rudely. And it was not purely a physical attraction, although there was plenty of that as well.

He supposed it was her determination, her independence, and the fact that she was so very different from any other woman he had ever met before. He could not help but admire how she tried so hard to fit in. Whatever it was — and no matter how odd it seemed to him, a determined bachelor — he knew himself to be unquestionably, irredeemably in love.

Sara's head pounded. She had never been in such pain before. But there was something else. A feeling of comfort, of warmth, of caring. Where was that coming from?

Ah yes, Reath. She was in Reath's arms. Cradled against his solid chest. It felt so good, she didn't ever want to move.

So she didn't, but snuggled down even more into her warm, cozy, sandalwood-scented haven.

"Sara, my dear, Sara."

The voice was calling from far away.

Sara wanted to ignore it, but it would not stop, and it seemed like it was getting closer.

Sara cracked open one of her eyes and her aunt's face swam into focus. She tried to sit up, but her head hurt like the dickens.

Her aunt gently pushed her back down on to the bed and replaced the cool cloth on her forehead. "It's all right, my dear. Do not try to move. You've just had a nasty fall."

Sara lay back down and tried to remember what had happened. She had been racing with Reath, Fungy, and Lord and Lady Huntley over the field toward the abbey. She had jumped a wall, but Reath had been calling out something to her when she had. She hadn't been able to make out what it was, and then her horse landed on a patch of wet grass and lost her footing.

She opened her eyes again. Her aunt was still there, looking very concerned.

She gave her a wobbly smile. "Is there anything broken?"

Lady Darlington gave a sigh of relief. "No. You are very lucky and only bumped your head. But you certainly had us all rather worried when you lost consciousness."

"I am sorry, Aunt Deanna."

Her aunt gave a little laugh. "It is quite all right. You just need to rest a little and then we'll try to get you home with as little jostling as possible. All right?"

Sara tried to nod, but it hurt too much. She settled for a whispered, "Thank you."

When Sara next woke up, it was to the sound of men's voices. Her head was still quite painful, but not nearly as bad as it had been earlier.

"I don't know what game you are playing at, Reath, but I can't say that I like it overmuch," Lord Alston was saying.

"I beg your pardon," Reath replied in a slightly offended tone.

"What is it that you are trying to do, assuage your conscience by doing the pretty to Lady Darlington's cousin?" Lord Alston said.

"I am not trying to do any such thing, I assure you," Reath said. He sighed. "And you might as well know that I am aware that Miss Whately is Wynsham's daughter."

There was silence for a moment and then, "How did you find that out?" Lord Alston asked.

"She told me herself, as a matter of fact."

"And did you tell her of your relationship with her grandfather?"

"I had no relationship with her grandfather," Reath sounded defensive.

"No? What would you call it then, when you play cards with a man and then walk away with all that he owns in this world?"

Reath did not answer right away. "I would call it a horrible mistake."

Alston humphed.

"On both my part and Lord Wynsham's. He should never have been playing if he could not stand to lose," Reath said.

Sara gasped. She could barely contain her outrage. If her head did not hurt so much, she would have gotten up and confronted Lord Reath right then and there. As it was, the sound she had made caught the attention of the gentlemen.

Lord Alston was the first to her side. "Sara, you are awake. How are you feeling, my dear?"

"Aside from a splitting headache, quite fine, thank you, sir," Sara managed to say. Should she let him and Reath know that she had heard their conversation? Something told her that she should not. She swallowed her ire but felt sick to her stomach.

Lord Alston gave her a little smile. "Your aunt just stepped outside for a moment, but she should return any moment. Perhaps after you've had a cup of tea, you will feel well enough to travel back to the city."

"Yes, thank you, I am sure that I will."

"Miss Whately, may I just say how happy I am that you are doing better. You gave us quite a scare there," Reath said, approaching the bed where she lay.

Sara bit her lip. It took a great deal of

concentration not to scream out all that she felt.

"Thank you," she ground out.

She did not even dare to look at him for fear that her anger would burst through her rapidly crumbling defenses. She had an overwhelming desire to scream at him, hit him, and cry on his shoulder all at the same time. Goodness, how her head pounded!

How could Reath be the same man who had stolen her family's estate from her grandfather? Reath was the gentleman who had been all that was kind and good. The one who had helped her out of so many difficult situations, made sure that she didn't offend important people, and had gently shown her how to behave properly in society.

He was also the one who . . . a shiver of excitement ran up her spine when she remembered dancing with him at her aunt's house, their bare hands touching in the most intimate way. And just this afternoon, she knew, he had carried her all the way back to the inn on his lap. She had only been half conscious, but she had known that it was him. Who else would smell of sandalwood and leather and feel so good to snuggle up to and rest her aching head upon?

And yet he was also responsible for all of her family's troubles.

She wanted desperately for him to hold her and tell her that it wasn't true, that he wasn't the one who had taken her family's estate, forcing her grandparents to die in penury and for her to live at the very edge of that sorry state for most of her life. But she knew that would never happen.

She had heard his friends calling him Sin, but she had never put it together until now. Sin — Sinclair Stratton. A name she had grown up hating.

And yet he was also the man she thought she loved. She felt so betrayed.

She felt a tear slide down her cheek, but quickly wiped it away. She would not cry. She would not show any emotion whatsoever.

So many times she had allowed her anger to get the better of her. But not this time. Nor would she allow her softer emotions to rule either her tongue or her tears. She closed her eyes and took a deep breath to control her wayward emotions.

Her aunt bustled into the room, followed by a maid with a tea tray. "Oh my dear, I am so glad that you have awakened. I do hope that you are feeling much more the thing."

Reath moved away from the bed to make way for her aunt. Had he seen her tears? Did he know what she was going through? She stole a peek at him. He looked concerned, but hopefully that was for her well-being, and not because she knew who he truly was.

Sara struggled to sit up and felt her head begin to swim once again.

"Please, I beg of you, Miss Whately, take it slowly," Reath said. "May I assist you?"

"Thank you, sir, but I believe I can manage," Sara managed to say through her pain. He put his arm under her back and lifted her easily into a sitting position, setting her down again very gently.

"Thank you, my lord," Lady Darlington said. "You will be kind enough to tell the others, while you partake of tea downstairs in the parlor, that Sara will be just fine." Her aunt could not have made her dismissal of him any clearer.

He bowed and left the room. Sara could not help but breathe a sigh of relief. She accepted the cup of tea from her aunt, and kept all of her focus on that while she drank the hot soothing liquid. She did not even trust herself to converse with her aunt just at the moment, her emotions were in such confusion.

Sara was never more grateful to climb into her own bed at her aunt's London home. The soft pillow against which she finally laid her aching head provided relief after the jostling of the carriage.

Annie placed a cold compress over her eyes and murmured soothing words. She had not treated her thus since she was a young girl and had just lost her mother. But then again, she had never injured herself so that she had to be cared for.

It wasn't just her head that was aching. Sara knew that her heart had been seriously hurt that day as well. But it would not do to weep and wail over a broken heart when there was nothing she could do about it.

All of the anger she had felt for the unknown Sinclair Stratton had slowly come welling up throughout the painful journey back to town. All of it she now transferred over to Reath.

Facts were facts — and Reath was a contemptible, detestable, damned unfeeling scoundrel. How she ever could have thought anything good about him was beyond her comprehension. He was lower than the scum of the earth — or so she told herself.

She wished she could be truly angry with him. She wished she could scream and curse and hit out at something or someone, but for some reason all she wanted to do was cry.

She would not do so, however. She would not! She took a deep breath and tried to relax. She wished that the pounding in her head would stop.

"I have learned today who owns Wyncort," Sara said from under the compress.

"Have you?" Annie did not sound very excited.

"Yes. It is Reath."

"Lord Reath? I can't believe it! What good luck!" Annie said with much more enthusiasm than Sara had heard from her in a while.

Sara pushed the compress up and off of her eyes. "Luck? How could this possibly be good? He is Sinclair Stratton, the man who won Wyncort from my grandfather. The man I have hated for the past ten years! I have been harboring a hornet in my breast. How can that be good luck?"

"Calm down, Miss Sara. All this ranting and raving cannot be good for your head." Annie moved the compress back over Sara's eyes and pressed her warm hand against her forehead. "I must admit, I thought he had more sense than to steal someone's livelihood, but perhaps there were circumstances that you don't know about."

Sara tried once again to relax. "Perhaps, or perhaps you just do not wish to think ill of him for whatever reason."

"I have rather taken a liking to the gentleman, and I think you have too."

Sara stayed quiet.

"Well, it is good to know who owns the estate now, nonetheless," Annie continued, ignoring Sara's silence.

Sara pushed her feelings for Reath aside and tried to think about this dispassionately. Was it good that she knew the man who owned the estate? Well, she knew where he was, and it wasn't at Wyncort. But then, neither was she. She still had to find a way to get back there. But how?

"Of course! If Reath owns Wyncort, then I can ask him to take me there." She snatched the compress off her eyes again and sat up on her elbow. "How stupid I am not to have seen this before, Annie! I can use Reath to get into Wyncort."

Annie smiled at her and took the compress from her hand. Rinsing it out with fresh cool water, she then encouraged her mistress to lay back down and placed it over her eyes and forehead once again.

"But how?" Sara said. "How can I ask without his becoming suspicious of why I want to go there? He knows that my father should be Lord Wynsham. I told him so myself."

"Why not just tell him that you want to see your family's estate?"

"No, that would be too obvious, and he might say no. No, I need to be more careful, more thoughtful about this," she said slowly.

Then it came to her. "I think I have a plan."

Twenty

When Sara came into the drawing room, she still looked peaked, but Reath was so relieved to see her up that he paid no attention to it.

"Miss Whately, I cannot tell you how happy I am to see you looking so well."

Sara smiled up at him as he took her hands. "Thank you, sir. I am feeling much better, thanks to your extreme good care."

She led him to the sofa and sat down in a way that it was obvious that she wanted him to sit next to her.

"Now was it my imagination, or did you not call me Sara after I had fallen?"

Reath was caught off guard for a moment, but then gave her a small apologetic smile. "I do beg your pardon. In my concern for your well-being, I might have inadvertently called you by your given name."

"You need not beg for my forgiveness. I would like you to call me by my name, and I shall call you Reath, if you do not mind. I am certain that calling you Sinclair would be much too intimate, would it not?" She smiled sweetly at him.

Reath felt his face relax into a smile. He felt drawn to her in a way he could not explain. Her behavior was much more kind and gentle than he had ever seen before. It was much more . . .

Reath sought for the word he was looking for . . . normal. That was it. She was acting like a normal female, not the strong, sometimes abrasive young lady he had come to know. Perhaps this knock on her head had somehow changed her.

"My closest friends call me Sin, but I believe Reath would be just fine."

Reath wasn't sure, but he thought she was batting her eyelashes at him. Either that or she had something in her eye.

"And is there a reason why they call you Sin? Some youthful folly — or your reputation, perhaps?" she said looking up at him from under her eyelashes, which she had now stopped fluttering.

Reath felt his lips twitch at her innuendo but he held back his laughter, certain that she knew nothing about what she was implying. And he was definitely not going to tell this young innocent about his sinful past.

"No, it is simply the first syllable in my name."

"Oh."

Was it possible that she looked disappointed?

She looked down at her hands. "You know, you have never told me much about yourself. I told you all about my childhood last week at my aunt's Venetian breakfast. But you somehow managed to tell me very little about your past. All I truly know about you is that you are a viscount."

There was something definitely odd here. Sara Whately had never even hinted that she was interested in him, let alone shown any curiosity about his life.

The hair on the back of his neck prickled, warning him that something was afoot. His instincts had never been wrong in this regard. And yet here was a beautiful young woman wanting him to tell her about himself and ready to hang on his every word. What more could any man want?

"What is it that you want to know, Sara?"

Sara shrugged and then looked up at him with wide innocent eyes. "I don't know. Tell me about your interests, your hobbies. Do you hunt? Gamble? Own race horses? Do you consider yourself more of a Corinthian or a dandy?"

Reath laughed. "I suppose I might fall

more into the Corinthian category, but I am no longer so much of a sportsman."

"Were you?" Sara asked, moving herself closer to him.

"Oh, yes, at one point in my life. Merry, Fungy, and I were quite well known for challenging other young gentlemen to races and other such tomfoolery," Reath said, beginning to feel rather warm. He looked over at the fireplace, but it was empty. The heat was not coming from there.

Sara laughed a sweet tinkling little laugh. "And did you win?"

"Of course! We always won."

"But you do not race any more? Why not?"

Reath thought about the last race he had run — he had won a race to Bath and back and had then taken his winnings to the card tables at Brooks. There his luck held out, but that of Lord Wynsham had not.

Reath forced the smile back on to his face. "I do not gamble any more. I suppose I lost a taste for it."

"I see."

There was an awkward silence. Sara smiled up at him again and said, "Then tell me about your estates. Do you own more than one?"

"I own three. Rathergreen is my family's seat. Then there are two other smaller estates that I own," he said, deliberately not naming Wyncort.

"Are any of them close to London?" She leaned closer to him. As she did so, the low neckline of her dress gaped open a bit to show her soft white flesh, which disappeared into the dark recesses of the fine white cotton bodice.

Reath swallowed and pulled his eyes from her bosom, forcing himself to focus on her face. It was indeed a lovely face, although there were two spots of color on her cheeks just now. But that only emphasized her full pink lips and her vibrant blue eyes.

Reath wondered why she was flushed.

"I enjoyed myself so much out in the country yesterday," Sara continued. "It would be lovely if we could do it again — only perhaps we could lunch at your estate instead of a public inn?"

Even knowing that she was up to something, Reath could not help but admire the beautiful, delicately feminine woman sitting so close to him. Her subtle scent of roses teased his senses, and he realized with chagrin that she was not smelling of lemons today. Her soft womanly body was mere inches from his hands, which he had clasped tightly against his legs. It would be so easy to reach out and . . .

He stood up abruptly and moved as far away from her as he could while still being polite. He knew that it was obvious that she had affected him. He rested one foot on the empty fire grate to hide his discomfort. Then he quickly analyzed the situation.

She was being much too transparent in her attempts. Reath suddenly felt as if someone had slapped him in the face, forcing him to wake up to the reality of the situation he was in. Sara was trying to use her womanly wiles in order to influence him.

Perhaps she had thought to be coy by asking about his hobbies and having that lead to his gambling. But when that didn't work, she had turned to asking about his estates. They both led to one thing — Wyncort.

Now that he allowed himself to acknowledge this truth, it was as obvious as it was painful to see. He was amazed at how hurt and stunned he was that she would do this.

Yet she was a woman, and she was simply using him to further her own ends, just like every other woman he had ever known. He felt betrayed.

He had thought that she was different, but she wasn't. How could he have been so taken in? His anger at her attempts to trick him was growing rapidly.

He had thought that he loved this woman. He had been planning on proposing to her this very afternoon. What a fool he was! She had played him so well, he hadn't even seen it coming.

"How dare you!" he snarled, not even trying to hide his anger. "How dare you attempt to use me! Your feeble attempts at using your feminine wiles will not work. Yes, you were convincing for a few moments, but you went too far."

He felt his hands clench into fists. He could barely hold on to his sudden rage. "Why, you are no better than the lowest light skirt! A trollop, that is what you are. You should be ashamed of yourself! Displaying your body to me, batting your eyelashes and practically sitting in my lap, as if you were trying to convince me to take you to my bed.

"Or is that indeed what you want?" It took only three long strides and he was standing directly in front of her.

Her mouth was hanging open, and her bright blue eyes looked up at him, filled with undisguised fear and unshed tears. Her entire face was bright red with embarrassment.

He reached down and grabbed her arm, hauling her up onto her feet. Roughly he crushed his lips to hers. How he wanted her. To touch that beautiful soft body she had been displaying to him just moments before. Reath could now feel his heart pounding, hear the blood rushing through his veins. He was filled with a desire that demanded immediate release.

Somehow reason still held sway in his brain. She was an innocent.

She had to learn, however, that she was playing with fire and she would get burned. He forced his tongue into her mouth and pressed his hard body to hers. But there he stopped. He did not truly want to hurt her, just to give her a good scare.

She pushed hard against his chest and he let her go.

"No! No, that's not what I want," she said, tears running freely down her bright red cheeks.

"Then what is it? Do you try to trick me into marriage? Is your aunt going to walk in on us at any moment to catch us in an indecent posture? Your maid is just sitting there, doing nothing. Not much of a chaperon, is she?"

Sara looked over at her maid, who was sitting in the corner quietly watching everything that took place, her mouth hanging open. Was that an apology on Sara's face? It was hard to tell through his anger.

"I must say, Miss Whately, I had thought you better than this. I had thought that you were different from other young ladies who were simply out to trick me into marriage for my money and my title. But you — you disgust me!

"No, do not argue with me. I know what it is you want. All you want is to get to Wyncort. How long have you known that it was I who owns your family's estate? How long? From yesterday? From a week ago? From the day I met you in Portsmouth? Was that deliberate too?"

He was shouting now, but he could not help it. The pain from her betrayal seared through his heart, even as he tasted the bile of his anger in the back of his mouth.

"You have played me for a fool, Miss Whately, but you will do so no more, I can assure you! Good-bye, Miss Whately. I hope I never have the pleasure of your company again."

He strode out of the room and then out of the house.

He flipped a coin to the boy who was holding his horse, mounted his curricle, and took off as fast as city traffic would allow.

He drove faster as soon as the roads began to clear, urging his horse on, and soon he was speeding down a near empty road. How could he ever have thought himself in love with that deceiving, conniving chit? He had thought that she was different from other women he had known. But she had proven herself just as petty, just as cunning and devious as the rest. She had used him for her own ends without a care to his feelings or thoughts on the matter.

He allowed the thundering of his horse's hooves on the road to drive all thoughts of Sara and her duplicity from his mind. Miles later, as his anger eased, he realized that his horse was nearly blown. He would never do anything to harm his prized gelding, so he slowed down and continued at a more reasonable pace until he reached a posting inn.

He did not pause long there, only to see that his horse would be properly cared for and another horse hitched to his equipage to take him to Wyncort.

Once there, his mood was not improved when he learned that when he was not expected, the caretakers had left the stable hand in charge and had taken themselves off to the local town for a few days. He sent the poor boy off with a fly in his ear to fetch the wayward Mr. and Mrs. Tate back to their duties.

Reath paced through the empty rooms of the house, for once happy at the lack of obstacles in his way. Slamming through doors and kicking at stray chairs and tables that had been left behind, Reath stalked from one end of the house to the other, upstairs and down.

How could he have been so taken in? He had loved her. Loved her! And she had used him.

It was obvious to him what she had been up to from the moment she had him sit down next to her. Why else would she have wanted him to sit there? It wasn't as if she had any softer feelings for him.

He wondered how long she had been stringing him along. How long had she been building up to this little trick of hers to make him bring her here to Wyncort? Had she tried to attract him from the beginning, by being rude? And when that didn't work, had she changed tactics and tried the direct approach she had used today? He did not know what to believe anymore, nor what to think.

One thing was certain — she did not know that he had followed her to Drury Lane the day she had met with the fence. So he still had that ace up his sleeve.

He knew why she wanted to come to Wyncort. Her jewels must be hidden here.

Reath started tapping on walls, listening for a hollow sound. He had no idea where they might be hidden, but surely that was what she was after.

Twenty-one

Sara's head pounded worse than it had after her fall. But still the tears would not stop. She hated herself for her weakness, but no matter how hard she tried, she could not stem the flow.

He had called her a trollop. He hated her more than she had thought it possible to hate another. And she deserved every bit of what he thought of her because he was absolutely right. She had behaved like the veriest hoyden.

She had cut down the neckline of one of her dresses so that it was nearly indecent, and then she had flaunted herself at him. She had tried to be coy and cunning, but instead she had been stupid and naive.

Well, she had gotten what she deserved — a torrent of hurtful words that removed once and for all any illusions she had about how he felt for her. And a harsh, hurtful kiss full of anger and heat, which still made her toes curl just thinking about it.

She had completely ruined any chances she had had to get into Wyncort. Why, oh why, had she not listened to Annie and told him, if not the whole truth, then at least part of the truth? She did want to see her ancestral home. And there was no reason why, if she had asked straight out, he would not have allowed her a visit. But no, she had to ruin everything by trying to be clever.

Now she would never get into Wyncort. What was she to do? She had not only lost the man she loved, but her only chance at saving herself and her father as well. Due to her stupidity, she and her father were destined for a life of poverty and unhappiness.

There must be something she could do.

She stood at her window, staring out into the depressingly sunny garden. Her mind was blank.

She could not think of how she was going to get to Wyncort. She could not think of anything but Reath's expression when he had said good-bye. He had been so angry. So wounded by her duplicity, as he had every right to be.

It was time for her to go home. There was nothing more for her here. All her hopes and dreams were gone.

Blowing her nose and wiping at her eyes with her soggy handkerchief, she sat down and wrote out her request to Mr. Mark

Seeburn, owner of the Seeburn Shipping Line. His American cousin in New York had been all that was kind and accommodating when her father had applied for her passage to Britain. Now she hoped that the British Mr. Seeburn would be as well, because she needed a berth on the next ship bound for America.

Sara opened her eyes. She must have fallen asleep. It was nearly dark. Only one candle was lit in her room, creating eerie shadows flickering on the wall. The house was oddly silent. She supposed her aunt had gone out for the evening.

Sara was glad she had not been required to attend. She could not face being in public after her humiliation that morning. Luckily, her aunt knew nothing of what had occurred under her own roof. If Sara thought she had the least inkling of what had happened, she knew she would have had to immediately leave her aunt's comfortable home. Sara wondered if she would even have the nerve to go home to her father if he found out what she had done.

As it was, she would be returning in shame, with empty hands and an empty heart.

Sara lay in bed for a time, thinking over,

once again, the horrible events of the day — but this time, thankfully, without the tears.

No, she could not go home this way. It would be too horrible. She must find a way into Wyncort. She could not and would not give up so easily. There *must* be a way.

She remembered the letter she had written, booking her passage on the next ship bound for America. It would probably be a few days before she heard back from Mr. Seeburn, and perhaps even weeks before the next ship left Portsmouth. That still did not give her a lot of time to find a way to Wyncort.

A chambermaid entered the room carrying a bucket of coal. Her face and dress were black with the stuff and Sara almost didn't see her because of it. She blended into the semidarkness and moved like a wraith.

Sara sat up. That was it! She could sneak into Wyncort in the dead of the night wearing black. No one would see her if she were covered in soot, as this girl was. Reath was in London so she had no worries that anyone would be there. She remembered, too that the caretakers were frequently absent as well.

It was perfect.

Why need she wait for an invitation? She could simply go on her own. She jumped out of bed, nearly scaring the poor maid to death.

"I am afraid I don't know your name," Sara said, softly trying to soothe the frightened girl.

"Betsy, Miss."

Sara looked Betsy over. Her plan was perfect. She was about the same size as the girl. Certainly there would be no problems at all. "Betsy, would you be willing to trade your dirty black dress for a lovely new dress?"

"Oh no, Miss. If'n I's had a new dress, people would think I nipped it! No one'd believe that you'd just given it ta me."

"Oh dear, you are right. Well, how about an old brown dress of mine? I have one that I don't wear any more. It is not as well-made as my new dresses, but the material is good."

The girl's face lit up. "I like brown. It don't get dirty fast."

"That's right. Would you mind trading with me?"

"But surely, Miss, you don't want this old dirty rag?" the girl asked Sara with wide eyes.

"Yes. That is precisely what I want. It is perfect for . . . for a trick I want to play on my maid, Annie."

"Oh!" The girl giggled.

Sara ran to her wardrobe and shuffled through to the back to find her brown round traveling dress. Taking it, the girl slipped behind a privacy screen and changed. It fit her perfectly, and she was more than happy to give Sara her dirty old black dress in exchange.

After the girl had happily gone on her way, Sara changed into the black dress and then smeared her face with soot from the fireplace. Except in the direct candlelight, she could barely be seen.

She then took out her little pistol with the mother-of-pearl handle. It had been a birthday present to her mother from her father just before her death. Sara had brought it along just in case. A young lady couldn't be too careful when traveling alone. She made sure that it was loaded before slipping it into her pocket.

There was only one other thing to do. She slipped a few pillows under the covers of her bed to make it look like she was there, sleeping. Unless someone looked very closely, no one would ever know that she had gone out. She was ready.

Reath settled into his bed with the only

book he could find. It was a book of household hints that Mrs. Tate had loaned him. He really had no interest in learning how to make poultices, but he also had no desire to go over the events of the day in his mind yet again.

He was tired and just wanted to sleep, but his mind would not stop returning to the image of Sara's beautiful, sweet face with tears streaming down her bright red cheeks. He hated himself for what he had done to her. She had not deserved such rough treatment. She certainly could have had no idea of what she was playing at.

Reath shifted uncomfortably in his bed and returned to the instructions for a mustard footbath.

He flipped the page. *Paste of Palermo: for the hands to use instead of soap to preserve them from chapping,* he read. He skipped to reading just the names of the recipes. Lip Salve, Lavender Water, Unction de Maintenon. Whatever that might be. Reath continued reading that particular recipe. *The use of this is to remove freckles.* Ah. He turned the page. *Rose Water, Virgin Milk.*

Reath slammed book shut. This was not working.

He got up and went down the stairs toward the library and the decanter of brandy he had left there earlier that evening.

The sound of glass breaking stopped him in his tracks. Someone was inside the library, although no light showed under the door.

He remembered leaving his glass on the windowsill just before going up to his room for the night. Someone must have climbed in through the window and knocked it over.

Very quietly, he moved toward the door, his bare feet not making a sound on the marble floor. He put out his candle and then eased the door open and slipped noiselessly into the room. Against the light of the full moon, which shone through the open window, he could see the silhouette of a woman.

Reath pursed his lips together and swallowed the curse that threatened to spill out. He would never have thought that Sara would go so far as to break into Wyncort! Well, he would teach her a lesson she wasn't likely to forget.

He moved silently toward her, knowing full well that although he could see her, she couldn't see him.

Unfortunately for his plan, he stubbed his toe on an occasional table that Lipking had brought in to try to fill up the room as he had instructed.

He yelped in pain.

A blast came from Sara's direction and suddenly he was in a great deal more pain.

"Oh, my God!" He collapsed on the floor and clutched at the same foot he had just hurt, which now was in excruciating pain.

"Reath? Is that you? What are you doing here?" Sara's trembling voice called out to him in the dark.

The sound of footsteps running down the hall caught their attention, and then Tate was in the room panting, an ax in one hand and a candle in the other.

"That ax is not going to do us any good unless you plan to cut off my foot! But come here with that light," Reath growled from the floor.

Tate leaned the ax against the door and came forward with the candle. "Thought I heard a gunshot, milord."

"You did."

" 'Oo are you?" Tate asked, finally catching sight of Sara.

"Don't bother with her! Get me some strips of linen and then go for the doctor," Reath ordered, shortly.

Tate began to do as he was told, but

Reath stopped him with a shout. "Leave the damned candle!"

"Oh!" Tate quickly lit a candelabra and then left on his errand with a backward glance at Sara, who was still standing by the desk with her small pistol in her hand.

"I — I am very sorry. Honestly, I did not mean to shoot you," she said, kneeling down in front of him. Through the blackening on her face, he could see that her eyes were still wide with shock.

Reath sighed but held back the groan of pain that threatened to escape from his throat. "I suppose I should not have tried to sneak up on you. I did not realize you were armed."

There was an awkward silence, then Sara cocked her head to one side and asked, "What are you wearing?"

"Indian pajamas. They are very comfortable to sleep in," he ground out. He then took a deep breath and tried to continue in a more even tone. "You will excuse me for not being properly dressed. I had not expected any visitors this evening."

Reath knew he must be flushing with embarrassment and wished that he had had the forethought to put on his dressing gown. It wasn't that the pajamas didn't cover him, they did — the long white shirt, open at the collar, came down to his mid thigh, and the white leggings covered the rest of him — it was just that the very fine cotton they were made out of still made him feel practically naked under Sara's direct gaze.

Twenty-two

Sara began ripping a strip of linen from her petticoat, not bothering to wait for Tate to return.

"No, I imagine you were not expecting anyone at this late hour. Nor did I expect to meet anyone here. Why are you not in London?"

"I had work to do here — matters which required my attention. Might I ask the same of you?"

"Oh, er . . . hold still." She began winding the cloth around his still bleeding foot.

Reath gritted his teeth to stop from groaning in pain.

Tate came back in with more linen. After handing the strips to Sara, he said, "I'll just go fer the doctor, then, milord."

"Yes, and be quick about it," growled Reath as Sara continued to wind the linen around his now throbbing foot.

After she had finished her bandaging, Sara did not look up from his foot. She seemed unable to meet his eyes with her own.

"Your reason for being here, Miss Whately?" Reath said, gingerly standing up on his good foot and moving to one of the chairs nearby.

Sara, too, stood and sat down gingerly at the edge of the other chair.

"I, er, well, I . . ." she began, still not looking him in the eye.

"Miss Whately, I am sure that you have an extremely compelling reason for being here in the middle of the night. Especially after your little performance this morning."

"Yes," she said, interlocking her hands in her lap. She then took a deep breath. "My lord, I . . . I am very sorry for the trick I tried to play on you."

Sara blinked rapidly a few times and then looked Reath directly in the eye. "I would never have done such a despicable thing if I had not felt strongly compelled to do so. My only thought was to get into this house — in any way possible."

Reath was impressed despite himself. He had been so angry with her over the game that she had played, and now here she was apologizing in the most direct and brave way imaginable. She truly was a woman to be admired, he reluctantly admitted to himself.

"Why could you not have simply asked?

I would not have denied you access to your ancestral home."

Sara gave a little smile and shook her head while staring down at her hands. "My maid, Annie, told me as much, but I did not want to believe you would be so kind. I am afraid that I wanted to think the worst of you."

"Why?"

Her eyes reached his once more. "Because of what you did to my family. I have hated the sound of your name for the past ten years. Sinclair Stratton has been synonymous with everything that was unjust and unfair in this world."

Reath winced, but could not argue with her. It was true. He had done a truly horrible thing, but it had been unintentional. He had to let her know that, he had to make her understand. But now was not the time for his confession.

It was time for her to tell him why she was there. He knew already, of course, but he needed her to be completely open and honest with him.

"When did you learn my name?"

"Yesterday, when you were talking with Lord Alston at the inn."

"You did not know it before then?"

"No. I think I might have heard Lord

Merrick call you Sin, before that, but I never thought anything of it."

Reath nodded. He knew she was telling the truth.

"Why did you need to get into this house?" he asked again. "It can't merely be that you wished to see your ancestral home."

"No. There is more than that." Sara stood up and took a piece of paper from her pocket. She handed it to Reath.

Opening the well-worn letter, he read out the most awful poem.

"A father knows what is best for his son,
He has lived many more years.
One should heed his father's words
    of what is to be done
and thus avoid many tears.

In the master bedroom, had you
    married right
You would have found the key to happiness.
In that great bed found heart's delight
My grandchildren begot
    to give you great success.

Your nursery, if you had heeded my word,
Would have been filled
    with the crying of babes.

Keep them warm in the night —
  you would have heard
Those who follow a father's direction
  the Blessed Lord saves."

Reath looked up. "Is this supposed to rhyme?" he asked, trying to hold back his laughter.

Sara snatched the letter back from him. "Yes. A poet my grandfather was not." She sat back down in her chair. "It was his attempt at communicating with my father, who truly is a poet." She opened the letter again and looked down at it. "Don't you see? There are directions here to a treasure in jewels!"

"How do you know this? Does he say so in another letter? What sort of jewels are they? Do you know any more details?"

Reath looked over at Sara, who was looking more and more annoyed as he questioned her. He softened his voice. "Sara, are you sure there are jewels here? I am sorry, but it just looks like a bad poem written by a confused, disappointed old man."

"No! No, it is not! My grandfather had told Papa when he was a boy about the treasure hidden in this house. My father forgot about it until he received this letter, and then he told me about it. It is the reason why I came to Britain — to find these jewels."

"Why did your father not come to find them himself, then?"

"He . . . he does not truly believe that they exist. He thinks it was just a tale his father told him to occupy a child on a rainy afternoon," Sara said, valiantly holding back her anger at being questioned so closely.

Reath persisted, however. There was more to her story and he needed to know it all.

"Then why did he send you here to find them?"

"He did not. He sent me here to marry. Specifically, he wanted me to marry someone wealthy. But I refuse to marry for money! When I marry it will be for love or not at all," Sara said with vehemence.

Then she added a bit more quietly, "But we need the money. The jewels must be here. I need to find them."

Reath kept a close rein on himself. Here, indeed, lay the deeper truth. He felt a great relief, knowing that she had told him everything.

And yet he did not want Sara to see the impact her words were having on him. Sara was so earnest and determined to do what was right and to help her father. She was keeping her anger at his prying in check and yet maintaining her independent spirit.

His heart went out to her and he yearned to take her in his arms and tell her that everything would be all right. The urge to hold her and protect her from everything was so strong within him. And he wanted to thank her for being so open and honest with him.

But he would wait. His turn to be honest with her was to come, he was sure of it, but first they had a treasure to find.

"I am sure that you will find your treasure." Reath stood up and then abruptly sat back down, stifling his curses yet again. He had completely forgotten about his injured foot.

Sara jumped up to attend to him, but he waved her away and tried again, this time not putting any weight on his left foot. He took a deep breath and then said as nonchalantly as he could manage with pain shooting up his leg, "Where do you propose we should begin our search?"

"*Our* search?"

"Yes, our search. You will allow me to help search for your treasure, won't you?"

Reath said, unable to keep a slight pleading tone from his voice.

A smile crept on to Sara's face. "Would you like to?"

"Of course! It is every boy's dream to search for a missing treasure. Why, I can't tell you the number of times I desperately wished there were one at Rathergreen when I was a child."

Sara laughed. "Very well. I certainly would not want to be accused of denying you your boyhood dream."

She started to move toward the door, but then stopped abruptly. "Oh, but what about your foot?"

"Ah, well, if you would just be a little patient, I will try my best to keep up. It would be too much to expect me to allow you to go off on a treasure hunt while I sit here and wait for the doctor."

"Oh, no, indeed. I would never do that." She returned to her chair and sat back down. "We will wait for the doctor together and then hunt for the treasure."

"Would you do that? That would be very kind. And perhaps you would like to take this opportunity to remove some of the very appealing — coal dust, is it? — from your face?"

Sara laughed and said, "Well, it was supposed to render me invisible. But it didn't work too well, did it?" Using one of the discarded linen strips, she scrubbed at her face, managing to clean away the worst of the soot.

"That is much better," Reath smiled through his discomfort as her familiar, beloved face emerged from its mask. "And, if I am not mistaken, I do not believe we will have to wait long to embark on our adventure."

The distinct sound of horses outside reached them through the still open window. Moments later the doctor, a dark ruffle-haired man, came striding in, followed momentarily by Tate. He had obviously dressed hurriedly, without paying attention to what he was pulling on, matching his tweed riding jacket with blue silk breeches.

He stopped on the threshold and looked about him at Reath, who was still standing, albeit gingerly, and Sara.

"I thought you said somebody had been shot and was bleeding to death," he said, rounding on Tate.

"I did. 'Is lordship were shot. I suppose the bleedin's mostly stopped by now," he said defensively.

The doctor scowled at Reath, who suppressed his laughter and then sat back down on the chair so that the doctor could attend to his foot.

The doctor came forward and pulled up the chair Sara had quickly vacated for him. "I rushed here to attend to a wounded foot," he grumbled.

Unwinding the hastily placed bandages, he examined Reath's foot, prodding none too gently and causing even more pain than there had been before.

Sara handed Reath a glass of brandy, but the doctor reached for it first, saying, "Ah yes, brandy, just what I need." He then poured it over Reath's foot, causing even more pain than his prodding had.

Reath was hard put not to scream or moan, but instead clenched his teeth together so hard that he was not sure his jaw wasn't going to break as well.

"You are lucky, my lord, very lucky. The bullet went clean through. It was a small bullet too, from the looks of it. From a pistol?" he asked.

"Yes." Sara took out her little pistol and showed it to him.

He took it in his hand. Turning it over, he said, "Fine piece you have here, Miss. Excellent workmanship. Where did you get it?"

"Excuse me, could we discuss the young lady's gun another time, and get back to my foot, if you please," Reath ground out through his teeth.

"What? Oh yes. Of course."

The doctor handed the gun back to Sara and then picked up the extra pieces of linen that were still lying on the floor. Winding them around his foot once again, he said, "Just replace the bandages every so often. It should be fine in a few weeks. Nothing really to be done. Such a small wound."

Reath slumped back against the sofa. The man had done nothing but pour some of his best brandy on his foot. But then, he supposed he should be grateful that he hadn't done any harm, either. Reath then got up and hobbled over to his desk, pulled out a small sack of coins and handed a few to the doctor.

"Thank you for coming out this late at night."

The man pocketed the coins, nodded to both him and Sara, and was shown out by Tate.

"Now, shall we get on with our treasure hunt, Sara? I think it will be vastly more enlightening than was the good doctor's visit."

Sara laughed and the led the way out of the library.

She turned to walk up the stairs, but then came back to him. Taking his arm, she wrapped it around her shoulders, saying, "Please lean on me, Reath, it will make it easier for you. I believe we need to go first to the master bedchamber."

Reath suddenly felt rather weak in the knees, but knew it had nothing to do with his injury. Both Sara's proximity and her kindness nearly overwhelmed him — not to mention the thought of being alone with Sara in his bedchamber. Lest she become aware of what she was doing to him, he quickly extricated himself.

"Thank you, Sara. You are extremely good, but I think it would be easier if I simply leaned on the banister for support."

"Are you sure?" she asked innocently.

"Yes, absolutely," Reath said quickly. Then, as if to prove it, he started up the stairs ahead of Sara, despite years of training which had taught him to allow the lady to go up first.

He led the way to the master suite and then quickly snatched up his robe and put it on as Sara entered the room behind him.

She ignored him, and went straight to the bed and began examining it.

"What are you doing?"

"I am looking for the key," she said, absent-mindedly. She then took out the poem and handed it to him again to reread for himself.

"You see, I've studied the poem and the only thing I can think of is that the key is hidden somewhere on, in, or under this bed. This *is* the original bed that was here when you stol . . . when you won the estate?"

Reath narrowed his eyes and raised one eyebrow. He knew precisely what she had been about to say. "I assure you Sara, I did *not* steal Wyncort. I won it honestly. Your grandfather should not have . . ."

"I do not wish to discuss that right now. We are looking for the treasure, need I remind you?" Sara said hotly.

"Very well. You feel the key is hidden somewhere on the bed. I can tell you that the mattress was aired before I came here, so it could not be there."

Sara nodded and stopped prodding the mattress.

The bed was a large tester bed with four posters, with balls at the top of each one. Sara began to look around at these and then exclaimed.

"That one, there. It is bigger than the

rest!" she said, pointing to the ball at the top of the poster at the foot of the bed. She quickly took off her little half boots and climbed up on to the bed, but she was not tall enough to reach the ball.

"If you would allow me?" Reath said, climbing up next to her, grimacing slightly as he did so. He reached up and unscrewed the ball and then handed it down to her.

Standing on his bed next to Sara put dreadful thoughts into his mind. Sara seemed to notice it too, for she flushed and then quickly jumped down and focused on the ball in her hand.

After examining it for a moment, she pried it open from the middle with her fingernails. One half had a leaf shape carved into it, while the other had the same shape protruding from it.

Her eyes lit with excitement. Bolting from the room, she called out, "Where is the nursery?"

Reath sat down much more carefully, and slipped himself gently back onto his injured foot before following her out the door. "Up the stairs and to the left," he called after her.

Reath joined her as she was examining the carvings around the nursery fireplace. An intricate pattern of leaves was carved into the marble, some standing out in relief, some carved into the stone.

"May I see the key?" Reath asked.

She handed it to him and continued with her search. Reath looked at the leaf carved into the ball.

"You are looking for an oak leaf?" he said.

Sara looked up. "Yes, but these all seem to be ivy leaves."

Reath joined her in her search for an oak leaf. "You start at that end, I'll start at this one. It would be more efficient if we work systematically, rather than both of us looking about randomly."

Sara nodded and crouched down to the floor where the carving started. Reath did the same on the opposite side, and they slowly worked their way up and toward each other. After a few minutes Sara exclaimed, "Ah ha!"

Taking the ball from Reath, she carefully fitted the protruding leaf into a carved one in the mantelpiece about a foot from the center. It fit perfectly.

But then nothing happened.

Sara stamped her foot in frustration and muttered some restrained oaths. Reath nearly laughed, but pursed his lips together to hold it back. Instead, he reached out and gave the key a little wiggle and then gently turned it to the right. A click was heard and a door sprang open just above the mantelpiece. It had been fitted so well into the wood paneling on the wall that neither one of them had noticed that it was there.

Reath could feel his own burning curiosity and could only imagine how Sara was feeling on this momentous occasion. He stepped back to allow Sara the first look into the secret cubby.

"Ugh!" she said after sticking her hand inside and then pulling it out again. "Spider webs."

Reath chuckled and put his own hand in and pulled out a little metal chest. He put it on a table and watched as Sara carefully opened the lid.

Twenty-three

Necklaces of pearls, emeralds, and rubies spilled through her amazed fingers. Loose diamonds, rubies, and emeralds littered the bottom of the box. There was indeed a treasure — enough there to keep her and her father from the creditors for . . . well, certainly for the rest of her life, if not for generations to come.

A giggle bubbled up from somewhere inside of her. A feeling of light happiness overwhelmed her, and seemed to fill up her chest. She felt like laughing and crying all at once — she was so happy.

She could barely believe it was real. She plunged her hand into the box once more, letting the glittering jewels clink so beautifully back into the box through her fingers. For so many months she had dreamed of this, hoped for it, prayed for it, and now it was here. It was here!

Sara looked up at Reath. He was looking so thrilled with her treasure. Warmth and happiness glowed from his laughing gray eyes.

Without a thought, Sara threw her arms

around his neck. "Thank you, oh, thank you!"

His arms instinctively encircled her waist. "What for? I have done nothing."

"Oh, but you have. You have allowed me to find my treasure and helped me to do so!" She stood on tiptoe and pulled him down so that she could hug his large form.

Turning her head so that she could give him a kiss on the cheek, she noticed that there was a strange expression in his eyes — they were softer and yet darker at the same time.

He bent down lower. Sara only had time to take a quick breath before his lips were upon hers.

He kissed her softly at first, but then he was nibbling at her lips and licking them with soft little flicks of his tongue. She opened her mouth to him and felt the floor drop out from underneath her as his tongue gently probed into her mouth.

Heat rushed though her body to places she had never noticed. Her heartbeat quickened. Tentatively, she responded, allowing her tongue to intertwine with his. His scent of sandalwood filled her senses and the taste of him thrilled her. She could not get enough of him.

She pressed herself along the length of

him and felt every inch, from his lips pressed against hers to his legs, which now straddled her own. His strength excited her. He was holding her close, one hand running down her back and over her bottom. He felt so solid and strong, his body hard where hers was soft. She pressed into him, wanting to get as close as she could.

But then his lips left hers and she felt bereft, but only for a moment. His lips and tongue seared a path from her mouth to her ear and then down the long column of her neck. Sara gasped as he pushed down the neckline of her dress and pressed his lips to the top of her breast.

He cupped her with his hand and ran his thumb back and forth over her nipple. Lightning shot through her body as his exhilarating touch made her shudder. Faintly, she heard someone moaning — and then realized that it was coming from deep within her own throat. She wanted more.

Reath took a step back from her but rested his burning forehead against her chest for a moment. He too was breathing hard, as if he had just run a mile. His soft hair tickled her nose, so she turned her head to caress her cheek against it.

But he moved away.

Holding her shoulders at arm's length, he shook his head, suddenly looking very stern. "No, Sara, we must not."

He took a ragged breath and then turned from her toward the door. "I am going to dress. You gather together your treasure and then I will drive you back to town."

The door closed with a firm click.

What had just happened? Sara did not understand. She had been so happy, and then he had kissed her. Kissed her! And she had kissed him back! And it had felt so good. But then he had stopped. Why?

Sara turned back toward the jewels still sitting in their box on the table. This is what she had wanted. This is what she had come to England for. This had been the one thing standing in her way of loving this man.

But now that barrier had been removed. She had found her treasure, and despite everything that had happened between them, she still loved Reath. She could not deny this feeling any longer. She loved him with all her heart. But he had left her and now all she had was a cold metal box full of jewels.

But what about what he had done to her family? She sifted her fingers through the jewels once more. If it had not been for him, she never would have needed to find these jewels. If he had not stolen her family's estate . . .

She closed the chest, took it and the candle he had left for her, and made her way slowly downstairs. She should be happy. She *was* happy. She had what she wanted. It was really too much to expect anything more.

Then why was the bubble of joy that had filled her chest minutes earlier now turned to a stone weight?

Reath splashed cold water on his face. He was much too heated from his encounter with Sara, and had to calm himself down quickly.

It was not right. He knew that. And yet he was amazed that he had been able to stop himself. Never before had he had to restrain himself from taking a woman. But then he had never been alone with such an innocent young lady before, either.

Even in his most dissolute younger days, he had kept a good distance away from unmarried girls from good families. He had not wanted even to come close to compromising a young lady and being forced to marry. No, widows, married women, and members of the demimonde were the only ones with whom he had cavorted.

But now he had thoroughly compromised Sara. Not only that, he had desperately wanted to complete what he had started. It had taken a great deal of willpower to stop himself. More than he had thought himself capable of.

She had felt so good. Her passion and willingness had fired his blood. It would have been nothing for him to lower her to the floor and take her right there and then.

But that was not how he wanted it. It was not the way to treat a young lady. And it was not the way he wanted to treat Sara.

No, he would do it properly. He would marry her and then make slow, passionate love to her — on their wedding night, in his own bed.

He stopped himself. What was he thinking! Married to Sara? Was he insane? He had been thinking of it earlier, but now the reality of it and all that marriage to Sara Whately implied hit him with full force.

Reath shook his head and began to dress himself.

Marriage to a woman who had insulted him in public, had the temper of firebrand, and the tongue of a shrew? He could not, would not even contemplate it. She did not need him any longer. Why should he put himself in a position where he was sure to get bruised, battered and embarrassed beyond belief?

And besides, she certainly did not love him, and he had decided long ago to marry only for love. His parents' disastrous marriage had convinced him of that when he was a young boy.

No, he was *not* going to marry Miss Whately.

But he was going to explain himself to her. He owed them both that much.

As they set off for London, the cool of the night air kept Reath's mind clear.

"Sara, I cannot tell you how happy I am that you have found your treasure," Reath began.

"As am I."

"However, I feel I should tell you . . . it was not my intention to keep Wyncort. I knew from the moment I won the estate from your grandfather that it was a horrible mistake." Reath paused, but found that he could not look Sara in the eye.

"I should have returned it right then or never accepted it in the first place," he continued, "but I was rash and flushed with the thrill of having won so that I did not think it through right away. When I finally had a chance to do so, it was too late and I was already on my way to India."

Reath turned to look at her. She was staring at him, her blue eyes wide open with shock. He turned back to the road.

"You must believe me when I tell you that I have spent the better part of three years trying to locate your father. I have had men scouring the colonies searching for Lord Wynsham in every town and village. When I returned to England, my solicitor informed me that he believed that Lord Wynsham had been killed by the red Indians because there simply was no man by that name living in America."

"No. There isn't," Sara said softly.

"No. I went to London and deliberately sought out Lady Darlington, hoping to learn from her her brother's whereabouts, but she put me off. It was not until you told me yourself that your father had taken his wife's name as his own that I realized who you were and where Lord Wynsham was."

"That is why you were so fascinated by my background. My aunt and Lord Alston thought you were up to something, but did not know what. You were trying to learn my father's whereabouts . . . and I inadvertently told you."

"Well, it was a good thing that you did. I have since written to your father informing him that Wyncort is his. I do not want the estate. As I said, I never should have accepted it in the first place."

"You — you wrote to him? To my father?"

"Yes. I hope the letter will reach him before too long. I must admit I am slightly worried about the growing hostilities between our countries."

"You are giving Wyncort back," Sara repeated. She looked down at the chest of jewels in her lap. "Then I suppose I don't need these. Not anymore."

Reath looked at the box. "No, not if your intention was to use them to buy the estate back. But if your father wishes to continue to live in Philadelphia, I am sure that the money you get for them will be very useful to him."

"It certainly will," Sara said with conviction.

"He might also need that money to bring Wyncort back to full productivity. Although the estate can support itself — indeed, it has been doing so for the past ten years through the excellent management of the bailiff — it could do with some modernization."

Sara nodded, but did not say anything. Reath tried, but could not discern if she was happy with his revelations or upset. If only he could hold her, take her in his arms once again, he might be able to tell what she was feeling.

Neither of them spoke for a while after Reath's admission. The sun was slowly beginning to peek above the horizon as they traveled through the countryside in his curricle. The day was going to be fresh and clear. Sara took a deep breath and filled herself with the clean, fresh spring air.

She did not know what to think. Her mind was awhirl with thoughts and emotions. She was stunned that he had been trying to give the estate back to her father. Amazed that he had felt bad about taking it in the first place. And finally, awed and a little horrified by the fact that if they had simply been honest with each other from the first, none of the tensions of the preceding weeks would have had to have happened.

Although if they had been honest with each other, she would never have come to know Reath as she did now. She probably never would have fallen in love with him.

The last barrier to her love for him had

fallen away. There was no reason to hate him any longer. Sinclair Stratton had redeemed himself.

Sara stole a peek over at him. He was looking very somber. His usual smile was not playing on his lips. If only she knew what he was thinking. Was he relieved that he had told her the truth? Was he angry with her or her father for using the wrong name and thereby making his search for Lord Wynsham nigh impossible? Did he love her?

Well, she supposed he had made his feeling on the last quite clear. He certainly did not love her. Perhaps he did not even like her so very much. Had he not pulled away from her when she had opened herself to him? He must be disgusted with her wanton behavior. First that morning, acting like a harlot and now kissing him so boldly and allowing him to touch her so intimately.

No, there was no future for her with Lord Reath. She should look forward to returning to Philadelphia, or perhaps she would move to Wyncort and learn how to manage the estate. That would certainly occupy her time and keep her thoughts from returning to her long and embarrassing days in London.

Yes, now she was free to do anything she wanted. She had money and Wyncort, both. She had everything she had ever wanted.

Except the man she loved.

"Will you sell your jewels here in London, or carry them back with you to America?" Reath's voice interrupted her thoughts.

Sara was actually a little grateful for his interruption, because her mind had been about to head off in a dangerous direction.

"I do not know yet. I haven't thought about it."

"In that case, you should give them to me for safekeeping. I will be able to sell them for you should you want to do so, and if not, I have a safe in my study."

"I am certain my aunt has one as well, sir." Sara could feel her temper begin to rise, but attempted to control it. He was being high-handed once more. How typical of this man that he would try and take over the situation.

"Are you certain of that?"

"Well, no, but . . ."

"Then you should leave them in my care. That treasure is too valuable to simply leave lying about."

"I was not planning on just leaving them

in my room, I assure you."

"Well, I am pleased to hear that."

"And I also know of a place where I can sell them."

"Yes. I would not trust that fellow on Drury Lane. He seemed very shady to me."

"And how do you know about that?" Sara's anger escalated dangerously. Did the meddling of this man know no bounds?

Reath had the grace to flush. "I followed you out the day you went to visit him. It was an incredibly stupid thing of you to do. You did not know who you were going to see, nor, I imagine, did you have any inkling of the danger in which you were putting yourself by going to that neighborhood."

"I cannot believe you followed me! Why you . . . you interfering . . ."

"I was not interfering. I was protecting you, you silly woman. You could have been seriously injured or robbed going into that neighborhood."

"In the morning? In broad daylight?"

"Yes, in the morning. Thieves and cut-throats do not care what time of day it is when they find a likely suspect. You set yourself up for disaster. And you should consider yourself incredibly fortunate that nothing happened."

Sara could barely believe the nerve of this man. Following her, poking his nose into her personal business. She was past simple anger. Luckily for him, he pulled up to her aunt's home just at that point.

"You, sir, will kindly keep from intruding in my life," Sara ground out through her teeth. "If I want to risk getting myself killed — not that I was — then that is my business. You are the most annoying, controlling busybody it has ever been my misfortune to meet. Good day, Lord Reath."

Sara hopped out of Reath's curricle with her chest of jewels without waiting for any assistance, and ran around to the side door of her aunt's home that she had left open for herself.

Her tears, she told herself fiercely, were tears of fury.

Twenty-four

After tossing and turning on his bed for a few hours, Reath got himself up and dressed once again. That woman was going to be the death of him. He was sure of it.

He could not understand why he ever offered to help her. What streak of masochism made him repeatedly attempt to keep her safe and happy? He had never been tempted to do such things for any other woman before. What had come over him? He had never received anything but grief for his kindness. She never appreciated his help in the least.

He walked over to Merry's, knowing he would find a sympathetic ear, and most likely two if Fungy was there as usual.

It took him most of the meal to detail for his friends just the events that had occurred the previous day and through the night. Appropriate guffaws and snorts of disgust accompanied his tale, and he felt a great deal better about the whole thing after he gone through the telling of it.

"Well, you are well rid of her," Merry said as Reath finished his tale.

"Good thing you weren't caught in such a compromising position," Fungy added.

Reath was silent. Yes, he supposed he was lucky. But why did he not feel happy about this? Or, at the very least, relieved?

Was it possible, even after she had blown up at him yet again, that he still loved her?

Merry laughed. "Yes, damn good thing, Sin! If you had been caught, you would be leg-shackled to a shrew for the rest of your life."

"Yes, I suppose I would," Reath said, slowly.

Merry and Fungy shared a look of surprise.

"Forever pulling her out of scrapes," Fungy said, narrowing his eyes at Reath.

"Hmmm." Reath nodded. He would be saving her all the time if he married her. But he rather liked that knight-errant feeling that came over him whenever he had to keep Sara from saying the wrong thing or doing something inappropriate. "But she would learn. Why, just look at how much she has learned already in the short time that she's been here."

"She has a very quick temper," Merry pressed.

"Yes. Have you noticed the fire that lights up her eyes when she is angry?" Reath said, feeling his blood warm as he remembered the look she had given him just before she had hopped out of his curricle that morning.

"Insults you at every turn," Fungy added.

"She has a very sharp tongue," Reath agreed. "Such a quick mind. She always keeps me on my toes." He laughed. "I never know what is going to come from her mouth — something sweet and kind or cutting and abrasive."

"She is short," Merry said in a last-ditch effort.

Reath smiled. "So fragile and beautiful and yet with a passion that nearly knocked me flat."

Merry shook his head, a smile tugging at the corner of his lips. "I suppose there is nothing to it, then."

Fungy nodded looking rather forlorn. "Going to have to marry her."

"Yes," Reath agreed, feeling the warmth in his body rise in the form of a smile on his face. "But will she have me?" Reath sat back in his chair and turned to his two best friends. "Gentlemen, I believe it is time that I start wooing Miss Whately in earnest."

Sara changed out of the dirty black dress she had been wearing all night long. While bathing herself, she looked over at the little chest of jewels sitting on top of her dressing table.

Reath was right. She had to put them into her aunt's safe as soon as possible. It was not safe to just leave them lying about.

But that would mean telling her aunt about them. How was she ever going to explain to Aunt Deanna how she came to be in possession of a treasure in jewels? It would mean confessing her activities of the previous night to her. She could never do that, she knew she just could not.

Damn! Reath was right again. She should have left the jewels with him.

Sara pulled her night rail over her head. What was she going to do now?

A little past eleven that morning, still much too early by normal town standards, Sara stood knocking on Lord Reath's door. Luckily, she was not too proud to admit when she had been wrong.

She had made a mistake — again. And Reath had been right — again.

It had been galling to have to admit as much. The more she had thought about it as she had tried to sleep that morning, the more she realized that she really had no choice at all but to go to him and admit her mistake. She was grateful that Reath wasn't the type to rub it in.

Sara could barely imagine what her life had been like before Reath. How had she muddled through without him? All of her life she had been so sure of herself and what she was doing. No one had ever told her that she was wrong. And to be completely honest, she didn't think she ever had been — until she had come England.

Reath had never had any qualms about telling her that she was wrong. And he was also just about always right when he stepped in and pulled her out of a potentially embarrassing situation. Well, all right, she admitted to herself, he was *always* right when he pulled her out of such a situation.

She hated that.

But somehow he always did it in a way that made her feel cared for, not reprimanded. He did not treat her like a child, he respected her for the adult that she was.

She loved him for this.

Sara was about to knock a second time when she heard footsteps coming up behind her.

"Sara, what the devil are you doing standing on my doorstep?" Reath asked, looking like thunder.

"I am coming to see you," Sara said, wondering why he was so angry and asking obvious questions.

Reath raised one eyebrow, but wasted no time in shuffling her inside of his house.

Once inside, he quickly pushed her, not so very gently, through the first door on their right. This was obviously his study. It had a very masculine feel to it, and it was a room designed for comfort.

He turned on her the minute he had closed the door. "Do you not know that young ladies do not call upon gentlemen? Why, anyone could have seen you standing there. Why did you not just send round a note asking me to call upon you?"

Sara opened her mouth and then closed it again. "I did not know. Why can I not call on you?"

Reath raked his hand through his hair, making a lock of it fall into his eyes. "It is just not done, Sara. It is not proper." He pushed his hair out of the way.

"Oh. But I realized after I got home that you were right. I should have left the jewels with you. If I were to ask my aunt to put them into her safe, then I would need to explain how I got them."

A smile flickered on and off of Reath's face. "I see. So you felt the best thing to do would be to bring them directly over to me to put into my safe."

"Yes." She offered him the chest. He looked so nonplussed that she could not help but smile. "I've gotten myself into another scrape, haven't I?" she said, laughing.

Reath tried to hold back his own laughter, but could not. "Yes, I am afraid you have. But this time, I do not believe I shall do anything about it."

"You won't?"

"No. I truly do not care if anyone saw you. I would not mind at all if you are compromised."

"But . . ." Sara was confused. Did he no longer care for her?

He took the chest from her hands and put it on the table nearby. Then, taking her hands once again, he looked deeply into her eyes.

"Sara Whately, I have tried to woo you and I had thought to do so again, but now I believe I am done with that. But I am not nearly done with this."

He lowered his head and kissed her. All of the feelings she had felt the previous night in the nursery at Wyncort came back with a vengeance. Sara wrapped her arms around his neck and went up on her toes to reach him better. Heat pumped through her as she pressed herself to him, reveling once again in the feeling of his strong masculine body.

He was not done, he said. He was not done making her feel so wonderful. Had he been forced to stop the night before?

But why?

His lips moved off of hers in order to nibble at her ear and the question slipped out before she realized it.

"Why what?" he whispered.

Sara moved her head so that she could see his eyes. "Why did you stop kissing me last night?"

A smile slowly spread across his face. "Because if we had continued, you would not now be the innocent that you still are."

Sara felt her cheeks burn. "Oh."

Reath laughed and ran a cool hand over one side of her face. "And I had to ensure that you got back to Lady Darlington's before you were discovered."

"So you did not really want to stop?"

His face became rather serious and his gray eyes smoldered with desire. "No."

Sara swallowed hard.

Reath took a step back from her and took her hands into his. "Sara, I don't ever want to have to stop. I don't want to stop rescuing you from scrapes and I don't want to stop protecting you and caring for you."

"I don't want you to stop, either," Sara interrupted him, worried that there was going to be a "but" following this. "I have always been the one to care for everyone in my household. I have always been the one to manage everything. But then I came here, and I . . . I don't know what I would have done without you. I promise to try to not insult you ever again — and certainly never again in public."

"That is good, because a wife should not insult her husband in public. At home you can insult me and rant and rave at me to your heart's content."

Sara felt her heart stop. "A . . . a wife?"

"Sara, I love you. Despite your lasting prejudice against the aristocracy." His eyes crinkled at the corners so that she knew he was jesting — at least about the last part.

But then she saw his eyes turn serious again — soft and deep and dark. He dropped to one knee as he asked, "Will you do me the great honor of becoming my wife?"

"Yes," she breathed. "Yes, I will."

And as he enveloped her in his warm, protective arms, she whispered with a smile, "And despite your high-handedness, perhaps I will even take your silly title — because I love you, my lord viscount."

Author's Note

I hope you enjoyed Sin's story. With four handsome and interesting men such as Merry, Fungy, Sin and Julian, it just did not seem fair not to tell each one of their stories.

Although the best of friends, they each have their own unique interests and troubles which leads them, each in his own way, to love. I will tell all of their stories in turn, although not necessarily in the order in which they happen.

Sin's story you have just read.

Merry was fortunate enough to fall in love twice, once with Julia Collingwood and again in *Miss Seton's Sonata*.

In my next book, *Miss Renwick's Revenge*, you'll learn the fascinating story of Julian's past and just how an Anglo-Indian came to London and became a part of the most exclusive segment of society known as the *ton*. In his quest for acceptance, he meets the beautiful and vivacious Cassandra Renwick, who has had some troubles of her own. Learn what happens when these two determined people meet — will they get their revenge or something much more?

Fungy, too, will have his own book, where this most unlikely of heroes will turn out to be the savior of a hapless bluestocking in *A Groom for Miss Grace*.

I do hope that you'll read along and follow the lives of these four men and the extraordinary women with whom they fall in love.